Grizzly Killer:
Smoke on the Water

Lane R Warenski

Grizzly Killer:
Smoke on the Water

Lane R Warenski

Paperback Edition
Copyright © 2019 by Lane R Warenski

Wolfpack Publishing
6032 Wheat Penny Avenue
Las Vegas, NV 89122

wolfpackpublishing.com

Paperback ISBN 978-1-64119-489-1
eBook ISBN 978-1-64119-488-4

Library of Congress Control Number: 2019930220

Dedicated to my father, Ralph N. Warenski
1912-1972

The man that instilled a love of our western mountains in me at a very early age. Whether hunting, fishing, or exploring the hills, his love of the west has been his legacy for me and my children.

Chapter 1

First Storm of Winter

HE WATCHED THE DARK storm clouds roll through and obscure the towering peaks just above him. Winter was nearly here; the first snows of the season were already covering the upper slopes. Today, once again, the peaks were being buried by a thick layer of dark clouds as the approaching storm moved in. Zach Connors, known throughout the west as Grizzly Killer, sat there on Ol' Red and shivered as the wind brought the first snow of this approaching storm down in to the valley of the Wind River.

Jimbo come out of the brush along the River, his head covered with the white downy fluff from milkweed pods that he had knocked open and his ears were covered in cockleburs. Zach couldn't help but smile at his large dog; at over five years old he still stuck his nose into every bush, hole, or crevice he came across.

It was late into the fall in the year of our Lord 1830 and the Wind River along with the Popo Agie was running very low; this had been an extremely dry summer in the Rocky Mountains. Zach wasn't looking forward to the cold and snow of winter in the Rockies, but he knew the coming snows were

1

desperately needed. The snow melting next spring filled the rivers and streams and made the beaver as well as the people in this harsh land thrive.

Trapping had been only fair this season; the late start this fall cost them valuable trapping time. They hadn't got back from their nearly half year journey to Saint Louis until the fall trapping season was well underway. Well, nearly back, he thought. He and his family were still almost two hundred miles from their home on the banks of Black's Fork in the Uintah Mountains. He believed if he and Running Wolf were back home in the Uintah's they would have many more plews than they now had.

He thought about his home often. He would never admit he was homesick, but he longed to be back there. He couldn't wait to see the big meadow with Ol' Red and the horses happily grazing on the knee-high grass, the little clearing where their Buffalo Hide lodges set, and the log dugout he and his Pa had built. Yes, he decided, maybe he was a little homesick. It seemed odd to him that he never felt that way when he and his Pa had left his childhood home in Kentucky. But he never felt the same way about the woods in Kentucky that he felt about this wild unforgiving wilderness of the Rocky Mountains.

Zach Connors was waiting for his partner, Running Wolf, who was working his trap line up a small tributary of the Wind River running into it from the northeast. As he watched the clouds rolling amongst the peaks, he thought back to when he and his father had first set eyes on these same mountains in the winter of 1824-25. They had made the terribly hard journey across the plains through that winter working for General William Ashley, and as they followed the Sweetwater River west, the majestic peaks of the Wind River Mountains came into view. Even though they had passed the Laramie Mountains with their peaks standing so high above the seemingly endless prairie and the Big Horn Range far to the north of where the waters of the Sweetwater join with the North Platte, these Wind River Mountains were the first they had seen up close with their peaks reaching for the sky, where the air was so thin no trees could grow.

At times like this, when he was alone with his thoughts, he still missed his Pa. Through most of Zach's life, his Pa had been his closest friend. He thought about the grave on Grizzly Creek that was his Pa's final resting place and remembered the bitterly cold, lonely winter alone after the big bruin had killed him. A prairie chicken flushed out right in front of his big dog and Zach remembered finding him as an abandoned pup. Jimbo and Ol' Red had been his salvation that winter. Working with the growing pup and big Kentucky Mule every day had filled his days with pride and joy as he watched the two animals learn.

Jimbo had grown into the largest dog Zach had ever seen, and even though Ol' Red had a stubborn streak, he and Zach formed a bond that was every bit as strong as the one between Zach and Jimbo. After five years, they were together most all of the time.

To most everyone in the Rocky Mountains, Zach Connors was known as Grizzly Killer, and Jimbo as the great Medicine Dog. The Indians believed Jimbo could read Zach's mind, and at times Zach was sure of it. The dog had learned fast to follow simple silent hand signals in obeying Zach's commands, but many times Jimbo would just do what he was supposed to without any sign from Zach at all.

Zach never had to worry about being alone again for now he had a growing family. Sun Flower, his first wife, is Shoshone, while Shining Star, his second wife and the sister of his partner, is Ute. Most of the trappers that know him believe he married the two most beautiful women in all the west and he agreed completely. Morning Star, his two-and-a-half-year-old daughter had become a particular joy in his life. She was born to Shining Star only a week after Gray Wolf had been born to Raven Wing, Running Wolf's wife and Sun Flower's sister.

Ol' Red's ears perked up, and Zach looked up the small creek where the big red mule was looking. He couldn't see anything yet, but then Jimbo took off in that same direction. A few minutes later Zach watched Running Wolf riding his chestnut gelding, picking his way through the dense brush toward him. Luna was not with him; she had stayed in the village watching over the two toddlers while Zach and Running Wolf checked their trap lines today. Luna was Running Wolf's beautiful white wolf that Jimbo had saved as a young puppy after a bear had killed her mother and siblings. She watched over the two children just as if they were her own.

Zach, Running Wolf, and their families were staying in the Shoshone village of Chief Charging Bull, the village where Sun Flower and Raven Wing had been born and raised. It had been on their journey to Saint Louis when they all found out that Sun Flower was going to have Zach's second child, and so on their return, they had decided to stay in the Shoshone village until after she had given birth and then return to their home on Black's Fork the following spring.

White Feather and Bear Heart, Sun Flower and Raven Wings parents still lived there along with their brother Spotted Elk, who was now a revered War Chief of the Shoshone. While Bear Heart, once a fierce warrior, was now a respected village elder.

Zach wasn't the only white man staying in the Shoshone Village; his long time and closest friends, Ely Tucker, Grub Taylor, and Benny Lambert were also staying with the Shoshone for the winter. Ely and Grub were older than Zach while Benny was much younger. Of the three, Benny was the only one married. His wife Little Dove was also Shoshone and the cousin of Sun Flower and Raven Wing from a different village. Little Dove's village had been attacked by a large war party of Blackfeet the year before and with Benny's help she had survived. The two of them have been together ever since that terrible day when Little Dove had been the only survivor.

Benny and Little Dove had accompanied Zach, Running Wolf and their families to Saint Louis, along with two close friends from Charging Bulls village, Red Hawk and Buffalo Heart, who were about the same age as Benny.

4

Zach had taken them on the long and dangerous trip into the land of the white man. He felt they needed to understand the number of white men that he was sure would eventually move west into the lands of the Shoshone and Ute nations. He wanted his family and friends to understand how different the ways of the whites were from that of the Indians, so they could live side by side when that time came, but that was for the future. Right now, in the winter of 1830-31, his only concern was trapping, which was his way of providing for his family.

As Running Wolf approached, Zach noticed he had another beaver hide rolled up and tied behind his saddle and nodded his approval just and a strong gust of cold wind swept through the valley. Along with the wind came a few snowflakes, and both men knew they could be in the first severe snow of this winter before they made it back to the protection and warmth of their lodges.

It was the beginning of November or Ezhe'i-mea', the cold moon, as the Shoshone called it. Most of the buffalo had left the plains south of the Sweetwater now and the elk were moving into the valleys escaping the deep mountain snows.

Before the buffalo had moved to their winter range, the hunters from the village had made a successful hunt, but like most winters, keeping everyone in the village fed required a constant effort. It seemed impossible to kill and dry enough buffalo to last the whole winter.

Sun Flower, Shining Star, Raven Wing and Little Dove were busy making pemmican. Knowing it would be well past the season of ripening berries when they arrived back home from their return from Saint Louis, they had spent time as they traveled along the Platte and Sweetwater Rivers gathering berries, nuts and acorns and dried them, then along with dried buffalo ground them all together. After mixing with rendered bear grease, they stuffed the mixture into buffalo gut casings. Pemmican would keep for months and provide the nourishment that was missing in their diets during the long cold months of winter.

Most of the other women in the village had already finished their pemmican by the time Zach, Running Wolf, and their families had reached the village of Charging Bull. With so much to do to prepare for winter, the four women were working nonstop, barely taking the time to nurse their rapidly growing children.

Upon reaching the Shoshone village, Zach knew it would take another seven or eight days to reach their home on Black's Fork and with Sun Flower pregnant and not feeling well, it was an easy choice for them to stay. Bear Heart and White Feather were thrilled, not only about having their daughters back home for the winter but when they learned their youngest child was going to have Grizzly Killer's baby, they were as proud as any Grandparents could be.

The four women watched the dark imposing clouds covering the mountains and wondered how much longer it would be before their men returned home today. All but Shining Star had been raised here in the valley of the Wind River and they knew how fast a storm could move in. The cold maker was coming, they could all feel it. They knew their world could look like a completely different land by morning.

Zach and Running Wolf were still over four hours from the village and they were supposed to meet Ely, Grub, and Benny on the west side of the valley on Willow Creek. Zach hoped as he kicked Ol' Red into a gentle lope that his three friends hadn't had any troubles. He didn't believe the storm was going to hold off long enough to get back to their warm lodges and if they had any delay at all, he knew they would have no chance.

The temperature was falling faster than the snow was when they met up with their three friends. Ely was riding out front as he usually did. His wound where he had been shot over a year ago had fully healed, but both Grub and Benny could tell he didn't have the stamina that he once had.

"If'n we's gonna beat this here storm, we best not take time to palaver none. Best get that mule of yours pointed south and a runnin'," were Ely's only words as Zach, Running Wolf, and

Jimbo followed the others at a steady gallop along the Wind River heading south.

Ely, Grub, and Benny had been out for four days now and had their big pack horse with them carrying all their traps and supplies. After nearly two hours, Zach could see the big horse was tiring and was pulling back on Benny as they rode along. He urged his big mule into a run and shouted as he caught up with Ely, "That pack horse of yours ain't gonna make it at this speed. He's 'bout to pull Benny out of the saddle now."

The snow was now falling hard, carried by the cold north wind, and they all knew this could mean a cold and miserable night. Ely pulled his mount back to a slow trot, but when he looked at the big pack horse, he knew that would never be enough, they would have to stop at least for a while.

Visibility was down to just a couple of hundred yards by the time Ely rode into a small stand of Cottonwoods growing on a bend of the river and stopped. The wind was now like a gale, blowing the heavy snow and stopping them from seeing the mountains even though they were right under them.

The wind had finished stripping the cottonwoods of the dry yellow leaves and didn't offer a lot of protection from the storm's fury. Ely yelled over the wind as he stepped out of his saddle, "We is gonna haft to wait this here storm out. Let's get some kind of wind break up 'fore it gets any worse."

Grub sarcastically shouted back, "Do ya really think it could get worse pard?" No one else said a word; they just went to work.

Running Wolf and Benny set a picket rope between two of the trees and tied the horses to it. Grub started digging a fire pit in the nearly frozen ground on the downwind side of a large fallen cottonwood that looked as though it had been struck by lightning and blown over many years before. Zach and Ely stretched another rope between two more trees and tied a buffalo hide to it, then staked the other side to the ground with the open end right in front of where Grub was working on the fire. With the wind blowing as hard as it was, the two of them were struggling with the hide until Running Wolf ran over to help while Benny finished loosening the cinches and unpacking their big heavy pack horse.

Once they had the buffalo hide secure, the wind was diverted enough that Grub finally got a tiny little spark to hold on the charred cloth and a small bundle of dry tinder he always carried with him lit. The thin dry shavings he had shaved off from under the surface of the small branch caught the flames as he skillfully fed the growing flames more and larger pieces until he was sure the gusting wind could not blow the fire out. The five of them huddled around the fire feeding it wood as the wind howled and snow started piling up around them.

Jimbo was curled up under the lean-to out of the wind, as Zach commented, "If it keeps up like this, we're gonna have to spend the night and this little lean-to ain't near big enough for all of us." Zach and Running Wolf had not been expecting to spend the night and their supplies were limited. However, both men knew they could never know what to expect in this unforgiving wilderness and never left their lodges without having what they needed to survive.

Two hours later, there were nearly four inches of snow on the ground and there was no sign it was going to let up. The wind was nearly as strong, but the snow seemed to be getting heavier as Zach and Running Wolf put up another lean-to. They had their buffalo hide bed rolls with them but no other hides, so while Running Wolf laid small branches onto the log they had lashed between two trees, Zach got on Ol' Red and rode over to the hill where he cut enough pine boughs to put a thick layer of them over the branches, making a good snow barrier for their lean-to.

Zach and Running Wolf each had a section of the fresh made Pemmican with them and they all had jerky, both elk and buffalo. Grub opened up their food pack and brought out their coffee pot, and as the light faded, they huddled even closer to the warm flickering flames, sipped hot black coffee, and ate the rich nourishing pemmican.

Chapter 2

The Village

LITTLE DOVE KNEW Benny and his partners were supposed to return today. She had left Sun Flower, Shining Star, and Raven Wing to prepare a meal for the returning men. As the snow fell and darkness approached, she realized they would not be back tonight. She wasn't worried, she told herself. Benny and his partners were experienced and could take care of themselves, but she was worried. She remembered well last spring when they had to leave their traps and run from a Blackfoot hunting party. She remembered her father and the other men in her village and knew they could take care of themselves too, but they were all dead now, killed when the Blackfeet had attacked. A tear escaped and rolled down her check as she wondered where Benny and the others were. She had to admit, she was very worried.

Sun Flower had been pregnant now for about seven months, at least that is what they believed, and had never been happier or more miserable in her life. She could feel Grizzly Killer's baby kicking and moving inside of her and she wondered if she would give him a son or another daughter. She had never felt emotions as intently as she did now. She wanted to be close to her husband all the time. She had started to hate these days when he was gone, and now tonight she couldn't stop the tears when she realized he wasn't going to make it back.

Shining Star was there for her. She knew what Sun Flower was going through, and as she watched Star and Gray Wolf playing in the warmth of their large teepee, she knew all the emotions and uncomfortable days and even the pain of birth was all worthwhile.

Raven Wing walked through the falling snow to the where Little Dove was and asked her to come and spend the night with them. She didn't want to be alone and gladly set the large heavy black pot outside in the snow and returned to the large lodge of Grizzly Killer.

They stepped through the entrance, and Raven Wing smiled when she saw her brother, Spotted Elk, was there. He had come by to see if Grizzly Killer and Running Wolf had made it back in the storm. It didn't surprise him at all that they hadn't; he knew where their trap lines were set. He told his sisters not to worry, that he was sure they had taken shelter to wait out the storm. He looked at Little Dove and said, "Cousin, the Blackfeet are just like the other tribes; they will stay in their villages for the winter except for a little hunting. You need not worry about them until spring." Little Dove knew that as well as the rest of them, but it still helped to hear it from someone like Spotted Elk.

Star and Gray Wolf, although cousins, had spent every day of their two-and-a-half years together, being raised as brother and sister. English was spoken in their lodge now, even when Zach was away. But with everyone else in the village speaking Shoshone, the two toddlers were sometimes confused which words they should try to say. Many times, it sounded like they were trying to speak a language of their own. The oohs and awes of babies mixed with English and Shoshone all at the same time. They seemed fine with one another but no one else had any idea what they were trying to say.

White Feather spent time each day with her grandchildren, and even though Star wasn't of her blood, to White Feather she was just as much her grandchild as Gray Wolf, or Spotted Elk and Butterfly's children, Yellow Moon, who was now four, and Roaring Bear, who was less than a year old and the youngest. Bear Heart, his grandfather, had given him that name the first time he heard him cry, saying he sounded like a little bear cub trying to roar and the name had stuck.

After their brother had left, the women were more quiet and subdued than normal, each one with their own thoughts and worries about their men. They all knew their men could weather the storm, but they also knew of the many other dangers they faced everyday living in this wilderness.

By the light of the small fire in the center of Grizzly Killer's large teepee, they took one of the large heavy buffalo hides they had tanned into a robe and started making their men each a pair of warm winter moccasins. The thick dark wool of the buffalo's coat to the inside and the tops of the moccasin coming nearly to their men's knees. Below the shaft of the moccasin, the boot part was triple layered for added warmth with each layer hand stitched separately. They were all happy to have something so important to do keeping their minds from what their husbands were going through.

*****

The temperature had continued to drop as the last of the light faded into the pitch black of the stormy night. The snow was nearly six inches deep with no sign it was letting up at all. Before dark they had brought several heavy round rocks from the riverbed and lined them around the fire. Once the stones were hot, they would hold their heat for several hours under their buffalo sleeping robes, helping to keep them warm through the night.

They turned in for the night as soon as the rocks were good and warm but not hot enough to burn their skin. Zach had two of the stones, one for his feet and one that he could wrap his arms around. As he felt the hard, warm stone, he thought about the naked bodies of his wives snuggled up on each side of him like they usually were and wished he was back in their lodge between the two of them right now.

They took turns through the night adding wood to the fire and by the time the darkness of the night was giving way to the light of the new day, the rocks they'd slept with were cold. They had succeeded in keeping the fire burning through the night and now they were all glad to get out of their cold beds and stand by the warmth of the dancing flames.

There was nearly a foot of snow, but it looked like the storm was nearly over. The wind was now light with mild gusts and the snow that was still falling was so light they could feel it, but against the white background of the fresh snow they couldn't really see it.

The horses hadn't had anything to eat, so they all started stripping bark from the cottonwoods to give them before they headed out on the hours long trek back to the Shoshone village.

Zach watched Ely moving much slower than any of the rest of them and knew the severe wound he had suffered from the murdering thieves had taken a terrible toll on his body. Ely was forty years old and Grub thirty-nine. The two of them had lived the life of a trapper in the Rocky Mountains since they were in their twenties. Both were proud of the fact that there were very few men that survived this life as long as they had. Ely was proud and stubborn, he could feel the cold was affecting him much more than it ever had before, but he just told himself he'd rather be dead than leave these mountains and the freedom that he loved so much. He knew he was moving slower now, and it took more effort to do his daily chores, but he had nothing but time. It didn't matter to him if he had to rest more often. The only thing that really bothered him was the deep-down ache that seemed to always be in his right shoulder where that round lead ball had torn its path through his flesh, nearly killing him, and the cold seemed to make the ache more intense.

Ely would never complain; he just accepted the ache was a part of his life that he would have to bare. Zach knew Raven Wing and her healing plants could help him if he would let her and hoped when they got back, he would drink some of her pain-relieving tea and would let her teach him how to make it.

By the time they were back in their saddles and once again heading south, the storm was breaking up. They could see small patches of blue sky showing through the clouds to the southwest. The snow was heavy and wet as many of the early season storms are and it was balling up under the horse's hooves. They had to stop fairly often to scrap the cold wet snow from their hooves.

*****

The smoke blackened tops of the teepees stood out against the backdrop of white snow, and it was a very welcome sight. They knew the fall trapping season was nearly over for another year. They would still trap until the streams and ponds all froze over, but that could happen at any time this late in the fall.

Neither set of partners had taken the numbers of plews they usually had by now, but they had enough that they were sure they could resupply for another year and there was still the spring season when the ice would start melting and the streams and beaver ponds would once again come to life.

It was just after midday when Zach and Running Wolf rode up to their lodges. The wet snow was now melting and the trails where everyone had been walking were becoming wet and muddy. Jimbo scratched at the flap of Grizzly Killer's lodge letting the women know their men had returned.

Little Dove was the first out of the teepee when she heard Jimbo and the horses outside. She ran to Benny and threw her arms around his neck just as soon as his feet touched the ground. Grub watched his young partner with his wife and then Zach and Running Wolf hugging their wives with a longing in his heart. It seemed to him the older he got the more he wondered about the choices he had made in his life. He had never wanted to be tied down with a full-time woman and neither had Ely but when he watched the happiness on his young partner and friends' faces, he couldn't help but wonder what it would be like to have someone waiting for him.

Zach saw Star and Gray Wolf standing in the warm lodge's opening, Star had her arms extended, wanting him to pick her up. Her whole face was smiling as he bent down and as he picked her up, she said, "Daddy" and then started talking to him just like he could understand the baby talk that it seemed only her and Gray Wolf could understand. It amazed him how fast his girl was growing. It seemed hardly any time at all had passed when they sat around the fire at their home on Black's Fork and he held her as a newborn during the naming ceremony.

Jimbo had gone through the teepee smelling everything, making sure it was still alright, then ran out into the village to meet his many other friends. The great Medicine Dog was loved by nearly everyone in the village and most believed his friendship was a very good omen. If the Medicine Dog liked you it made your medicine stronger.

Today Jimbo's first stop was to Red Hawk and Buffalo Heart who were out with the horses. The two of them were breaking a couple of two-year-old colts. They planned to have them both as good mounts before spring. After he received his ear rubs from them it was off to see Spotted Elk and Butterfly and their little ones. Yellow Moon was always glad to wrap her little arms around the two-hundred-pound dog, as was her mother. Butterfly would always remember the day he had saved her from the Frenchman, Jean Luč Lamont. Each time Jimbo came to her she would kneel down and hug him and feel the turquoise stone that she had given him. She believed that as long as the great Medicine Dog had the turquoise, he would protect her family just as if they were his own.

There were chores to do before any of the men could rest. Ol' Red and the horses had to be unpacked and rubbed down, then taken out to the herd where hopefully they could get enough grass to fill their empty bellies. The green plews had to be stretched onto willow frames and all of the wet gear and robes set out to dry.

14

Sun Flower and Shining Star started right in helping Zach, but Sun Flower struggled. Zach made her stop; he was worried and she looked pale to him and he could tell she was in a lot of pain as she tried to bend over. Sun Flower was a small woman with not much room to carry their child and her belly was already so extended with the growing baby she looked as if she was ready to give birth. The weight of the baby had her back aching nearly continuously with the only relief being when either Zach or Shining Star would rub it. She had watched Raven Wing and Shining Star go through their pregnancies but had never realized just how hard carrying a baby for nine months really was.

After the chores were all done and Star was napping in the warmth of the buffalo robes on the floor of the teepee, Zach laid down by his wives and rubbed Sun Flower's aching back. It felt good to be back in their warm embrace and wondered why neither Ely nor Grub had ever taken a wife. He knew there were many Indian women that would be happy to be with either one of them.

He heard Sun Flower's deep, heavy breathing and knew she had fallen asleep. He then felt Shining Star reach her hand under his buckskin shirt, running her fingers teasingly over his chest. He rolled over to face her, and she kissed him a long and passionate kiss. They made love there in the warmth of the teepee knowing both Star and Sun Flower were asleep.

That evening, just as Shining Star was getting a pot ready to boil some jerky, Spotted Elk came by and brought them a large Elk roast. He had led a small hunting party up the canyon of the Popo Agie that morning and they had taken two cows. The fresh meat was appreciated by them all.

It was too cold for them to want to eat outside, so after the roast had cooked on the spit over the fire. They all cut enough off for a meal and sat around the warm fire inside their teepees.

Running Wolf, Raven Wing, and little Gray Wolf ate as they always did in Grizzly Killer's teepee and while eating Zach talked to Raven Wing about the constant ache that Ely seemed to always have to put up with.

After they ate, she got her medicine kit and one of their tin cups. After putting in several pinches of different dried plants, she took out her small grinding stones and ground some aspen bark into a fine powder and added it, then added boiling water, making a hot herbal tea. After letting it steep until the cup had barely cooled enough to handle, she left and carried the tea to Grub and Ely's teepee. Ely didn't argue with her at all. His shoulder had ached terribly ever since this last storm had moved in. Raven Wing smiled at the expression on his face when he took the first sip of the hot bitter tea and said, "I know it's bitter, but it will help and make it easier for you to sleep tonight." Ely smiled and nodded then took another sip of the bitter brown liquid. Right after Raven Wing left, Grub looked at Ely and asked, "Lookin' at yer face, Pard that must be somethin' awful."

"Well, I tell ya, it sure ain't like a good cup of coffee." Ely replied. Grub shook his head and shuttered at the thought of drinking it.

The next morning, Ely felt better than he had in weeks; the ache was gone. As he had laid down for the night, he'd slept without waking even once because of his shoulder. Grub poured him a cup and as he sipped the hot black coffee said, "This here coffee sure tastes better than that tea did last night, but I tell ya, Grub, I ain't slept that good in a coons age and this here shoulder don't hurt none this mornin'."

Just then they heard a commotion in the village, then they heard Red Hawk's voice over all of the commotion as he yelled, "Grizzly Killer, the horses are gone."

Chapter 3

Stolen Horses

THE HORSE HERD had been split into three small groups and each group moved to where the wind had blown off much of the snow, exposing the dry grass. None of the blown off areas were large enough for the whole herd, so they'd had no choice but to split the horses up into smaller groups.

No one expected any other tribes would be out raiding this time of the year, especially with the way the storm had viciously blown in, so no guards had been posted through the cold night. Zach stepped out of his teepee thinking they had just wandered off to find protection from the wind, or maybe a pack of wolves had run them off. Just as he looked into the worried face of his young friend, Spotted Elk rode up and said, looking right at Zach, "Brother, they got the herd with all of your horses. The tracks show they are being herded east. It must be Cheyenne or Lakota; the Crow or Blackfeet I believe would have headed north.

Zach expression changed to one of real concern. Running Wolf, Benny, Ely, and Grub, as well as the women, had all heard what Spotted Elk had said. The only horses any of them had left was their riding mounts that they kept tied by their lodges. Zach never tied his big mule, Ol' Red never wandered very far and even if he did Jimbo would bring him back.

This morning was no different. Although he couldn't see the mule from where he was standing, when he called his name Ol' Red's bray could be heard all through the village and he came trotting right to Zach from the far side of Grub and Ely's teepee.

Within minutes they were all saddled and ready to ride except Running Wolf; Zach asked him to stay and protect their families just in case this was a trick to get the warriors away from the village. Running Wolf nodded. Although he wanted to go with them, he knew it was more important to protect the women and children.

Spotted Elk had sent Buffalo Heart on ahead to see if he could determine where the horse thieves might be driving the herd. He was hoping they would be able to cut the thieves off rather than just follow their trail. For right now all they could do was follow what appears to be a trail left by nearly eighty running horses that was now several hours old.

Zach was well aware that the Sioux, Cheyenne, and Arapaho were all longtime enemies of the Shoshone, but what didn't make any sense to any of them is why any of the tribes would be raiding for horses in the land of the Shoshone this time of year.

Buffalo Heart had taken two extra mounts with him and was pushing his horses hard. Although he had less than an hour lead on the rest of them, he was nearly ten miles ahead and was extending that lead rapidly.

Buffalo Heart and Red Hawk were both nineteen years old, the same age as Benny, and had been close friends of Zach and his family for over five years. They both had gone to Saint Louis with them and now, after being back home for only a few weeks, they once again had taken their place among the village as respected warriors. They both were excellent horseman. With Buffalo Heart being somewhat smaller, Spotted Elk thought he would not tire his mount quite as quickly.

He changed mounts every few miles as he rode not even stopping to do so, simply jumping from one horse to the next.

He was about fifteen miles east of the village when he could see by the tracks he was following the thieves were slowing down and making a gradual turn to the south toward the Sweetwater River. When he reached where the horses had crossed the river, he stopped to better examine the tracks. The mud around the tracks edges had already frozen, letting him know they were still several hours ahead. He realized then that recovering the stolen horses was going to take much longer than any of them had hoped.

Buffalo Heart looked across the river and the trail was now heading east by a little south, right toward the rising sun. The snow wasn't nearly as deep here as it had been back in the village and the nearly eighty horses had left a muddy swath nearly fifty yards wide. He wondered if the thieves would be simply running or if they may be setting up an ambush for he was sure they would be expecting the Shoshone to follow.

Zach was riding alongside Spotted Elk with Jimbo well out in front of them as they approached the Sweetwater. He figured they were now over thirty miles from the village and had been riding hard for most of that distance. They stopped there, and it was Red Hawk that first spotted the small pile of rocks Buffalo Heart had left.

The rocks were more than just a marker; the Shoshone used them as signals depending on how they were piled and these rocks told of danger ahead. As Zach saw the rocks, his first thought was the same as Buffalo Hearts as he said, "Ambush. Buffalo Heart believes they are leading us into an ambush."

Spotted Elk was silent for a minute, then slowly nodded saying, "I do not know who we are following but I believe Buffalo Heart is right. We will not ride blindly into their trap. We will wait here until Buffalo Heart comes back."

There were seventeen Shoshone warriors along with Zach, Grub, Ely and Benny following Spotted Elk, and many of the young Shoshone shouted their displeasure about waiting, believing their medicine was stronger than that of their enemies. It was Otter, one of the older warriors that said, "Yes,

19

our medicine is strong. It is strong because we have wise leaders that will not blindly lead us into trouble."

It was Howling Dog that answered, "But we have Grizzly Killer riding with us. Everyone knows he cannot be defeated; his medicine is stronger than all others. With Grizzly Killer with us, we cannot be defeated!"

Zach looked at the young man and shook head saying, "Howling Dog, I have never been defeated because I have never foolishly charged into a fight I could not win. Spotted Elk has proven time and time again that he can defeat the enemies of the Shoshone, not because his medicine is stronger than theirs, but because he is smarter than they are. Our enemies are strong, or they would not have come to our village to steal our horses." Howling Dog now looked confused. Was Grizzly Killer really afraid to go forward? He shouted, "I am not afraid, even if the great Grizzly Killer is!" A deadly silence fell over all of the warriors, even the horses were silent, as Howling Dog realized he had just called Grizzly Killer a coward.

Zach slowly walked toward Howling Dog. All the others cleared a path right to the young man, many of them was sure they were watching Howling Dog's last moments. Not a warrior among them believed he had a chance against Grizzly Killer.

Zach could see the fear in the young man's eyes, but he was too proud to back down. Everyone would know he was no coward, even it meant his life. Zach knew Howling Dog would fight, but he had no intention of fighting or hurting the young man. He stopped and reached out and stroked the neck of Howling Dog's horse, then looked up at the nervous young warrior and asked, "Howling Dog, do you believe I am a coward?" Howling Dog looked down and shook his head. He was ashamed for what he had shouted in excitement and anger, for he, like everyone else there, believed Grizzly Killer was the greatest of warriors. Zach continued, "It takes more than the lack of fear to be a great warrior; you must be strong like the bear, patient like the hawk, leery like an old buck and cunning

20

like the coyote, but most of all you must be wise like our grandfathers that have gone before us." Everyone there nodded as Zach turned to walk back to Ol' Red. He didn't expect an apology from Howling Dog; he knew the young warrior's pride had been hurt enough. He also knew these proud young warriors needed to be reined in from time to time so the older, wiser leaders could do their duty for the tribe.

*****

Buffalo Heart continued pushing ever farther ahead of Zach, and the Shoshone as he followed the trail to the east. The farther east he rode the less snow was on the ground. He still had no idea who he was following, but to him it made no difference at all. Whoever it was had wronged the Shoshone and not only would they get their horses back, they would exact the revenge the thieves deserved.

By late afternoon, there was only a skiff of snow left on the ground and he could feel all three of his mounts were getting tired and he knew he must back off the pace he had kept up all day. From the tracks of the horse herd he could tell they were now only an hour or maybe a little more ahead. He knew by the amount of ground he had covered this day that the horses in the herd in front of him had to be extremely tired and he slowed even more figuring the thieves would be stopping soon to let the horses rest and graze.

Buffalo Heart had rode nearly seventy miles in less than half the time it had taken the sixteen Cheyenne warriors that had made the daring raid against the Shoshone village. He was amazed the thieves had come so far pushing the nearly seventy horses in front of them, but he knew they must stop soon. The creek with dirty water was not far ahead and from the tracks it appeared to him they were heading for where that creek runs through the gap in the red hills, giving the water a reddish muddy tint.

He could see the land rising slightly forming the ridgeline on the west side of the Muddy Creek that was now only a couple miles in front of him. He then turned south, off the trail he had been following all day toward the red hills just south of him. Believing the thieves would be watching their back trail if they did stop, he did not want to be seen.

Staying behind what cover he could, Buffalo Heart covered the two miles in just a few minutes, then worked his way up the western end of the red ridge and down the other side. He reached the west fork of Muddy Creek about two miles west of the gap and stopped to let his three horses drink their fill. He then proceeded leaving two of the horses there he headed down toward the south end of the gap.

He was over a half mile from the gap when he first saw the horse herd. Buffalo Heart left his mount tied to the thick brush along the creek and proceeded on foot. He wanted to know who had taken them. There was only one warrior watching the horses and Buffalo Heart could tell immediately he was Cheyenne and he had to control his anger to keep from killing him. He could also tell the horses were exhausted and even the one guard wouldn't have been necessary. Then he saw a slight movement above the creek in the gap and he knew these Cheyenne were waiting to ambush the Shoshone they were sure would follow them through the muddy gap.

Buffalo Heart was nearly as tired as his mounts were as he headed back to his horse, making sure he couldn't be seen, he worked his way back to his other mounts. From there he headed northwest until he hit the wide trail he had been following all day, then proceeded at a pace he thought his tired mounts could handle back toward the rest of the Shoshone.

*****

Although Zach was and always had been a patient man, with this he was no different from the more excitable young warriors—he didn't like waiting. After three hours had passed, and the horses were well rested, they all knew the thieves were much further ahead of them than they had thought. It was either that or something had happened to Buffalo Heart for him to have not returned.

Spotted Elk walked back to where his white bother was talking with Benny, Otter, and Red Hawk and said, "You don't think Buffalo Heart would have tried something on his own, do you?"

Zach shook his head, but it was Red Hawk that said, "Buffalo Heart would never be so foolish and he would never let himself be seen. No, who we are following must be a great distance from us."

Spotted Elk nodded his agreement and said, loud enough for all to hear, "Let's ride."

They stayed at a fast lope until late afternoon then stopped to give the horses a break once they hit Cottonwood Creek. It was here that Red Hawk saw his friend Buffalo Heart leading his two spare mounts only a mile ahead riding toward them.

Buffalo Heart slid off his exhausted mount and while looking at Spotted Elk he said, loud enough so everyone could hear, "It is Cheyenne, I could not see how many there are, but they have our horses on the south side of the gap in the red ridge and they are waiting for us in the gap. I went over the red ridge to the west and down the west fork of the creek, so they could not see me."

All of the older, more experienced of them knew just where Buffalo Heart was describing; some of the younger ones had never traveled this far toward the territories of their enemies, the Cheyenne and Arapaho. This time of year, sunset was now less than an hour away and with the clear sky, the temperature had already started to fall.

Zach looked at the faces of the anxious young men and then at Spotted Elk, saying, "Brother, we cannot find and attack them in the dark. Right here, we are far enough away they will not be able to see our fires. There is feed for our horses and good water. If we leave three or four hours before sunrise, we can be in a position to attack them from the south. They will have no warning." Spotted looked at Otter who put his hand on Zach's shoulder as he said, "Grizzly Killer didn't mention it, but I would not expect them to have fires tonight; it may give their location away. After waiting all night in the cold they may not be in the mood for a fight come daylight."

Grub and Ely were both glad the decision was made to stay here at least for most of the night. Especially Ely; he was weary. He still wouldn't admit it out loud, but he was now realizing he just could not keep up with the younger men any longer. "*Hell*," he thought, "*I can't even keep up with Grub anymore.*"

With nearly an hour of light left, three hunters went up stream and three more downstream, all armed with only a bow and arrows to try to find some game. They had left in such a hurry only a few of them were carrying jerky and pemmican, but not enough to go around. The deer were in the middle of their rut, and they all hoped that would help the hunters get close enough they would have fresh meat.

There were four fires burning when the first hunter came back from downstream, but they had not seen anything except a coyote running through the short sage way out of range. It wasn't until all traces of daylight was gone that the group came riding in from upstream with an ewe and lamb mountain sheep across their horses.

It took only minutes for strips of the mutton to be roasting on sticks over the fires. Ely sat with his legs crossed next to the fire Benny had made. His bed roll wrapped around his shoulders, keeping the cold air at bay. Grub watched him and wished he'd brought their coffee pot and some herbs Raven Wing had given him. He was sure a cup of the warm bitter tea would help his lifelong friend on this cold night.

Zach guessed they had about three hours until it would be light enough to see, when they mounted up and followed Buffalo Heart into the starlit night. He followed the same trails he'd used just hours before as he guided the nineteen Shoshone warriors and four white men around and over the west end of the red ridge.

The sixteen Cheyenne were all young warriors that wanted to make one more raid against their enemies before the cold maker covered the land with ice and snow for the winter. They didn't know when they made their raid that many of the horses they had stolen belonged to the great white warrior Grizzly Killer.

Earlier this year, four of this same group had tried to steal his horses just south of the river the white man calls the North Platte, and as a result they had left several of their friends on burial scaffolds on a hill just south of the River. They had all heard many stories of Grizzly Killer and his Great Medicine Dog. They knew a year or two ago other Cheyenne from their tribe had captured Grizzly Killer only to be killed by him, his mule, and dog. Tonight, however, all sixteen of them were confident in their own medicine. They believed they would defeat any of the Shoshone that dared follow them.

Chapter 4

The Cheyenne

ZACH WATCHED as the first hint of light started to lighten the black sky just above the eastern horizon. Benny, Red Hawk, and Buffalo Heart, along with five other warriors, were in place high above the gap where the Cheyenne Warriors were waiting.

Spotted Elk had taken the rest of the Warrior's way out around to the south of the horse herd and were nearly in place on the east side of the gap. Grub and Ely had stayed down on the creek to find and eliminate the guard or guards around the horses.

The two old trappers had split up and were working their way around the horses in opposite directions. They hoped to have the Cheyenne guards out of the way before the fight got started so they could not stampede the herd. Not five minutes after they split up, Ely saw a warrior on horseback slowly riding straight towards him. Ely couldn't move without giving his position away. He hoped his dirty fringed buckskin jacket and wolf's hide hat would blend in good enough he wouldn't be seen.

In the dim light of the quarter moon, he couldn't see well enough to tell how the Cheyenne was armed. He knew a gunshot from either of them would spoil the surprise Grizzly Killer and Spotted Elk's had planned.

Ely was lying in short grass and brush as the Cheyenne approached. At about ten yards away Ely could see he was armed with a lance carried in his right hand and had a bow resting around his neck and shoulder. The Warrior was looking out over the horse herd as he walked on by Ely, who was only about five feet from him. As the Cheyenne walked past, Ely carefully pushed off the ground coming up to his knees. The Cheyenne's mount threw his head around and whinnied just as Ely threw his tomahawk. He threw the sharp hawk with all his strength, pulling severely on the scars of his wounded shoulder. Unwillingly he let out a grunt as he released the handle of the hawk, warning the Cheyenne. The warrior dove to the side, off his horse, making Ely's throw miss the center of his back but tearing a nasty gash from his shoulder nearly to his right elbow.

The Cheyenne landed hard but rolled to his feet. Ely reached for his knife. Even though he had a pistol tucked in his belt alongside his knife, he still didn't want to fire a gun. The safety of them all depended on this being a surprise attack. As Ely reached, he felt his hand on the knife handle but as he tried to pull the blade free, his fingers would not close around the handle.

The Indian was bleeding severely; the blood running down his side. He was holding a stone war club in his left hand and a knife in his right, ignoring the wound and bleeding as he started toward Ely. He was coming slowly and cautiously, not knowing there was anything wrong with this enemy before him.

Ely tried to make a fist, trying everything to get his fingers working, he could tell something had torn loose in his shoulder as he threw the hawk, and his fingers felt numb. His arm seemed to be working but not his hand. He quickly pulled the pistol with his left hand and as he did the warrior charged. Ely pulled the trigger, but the pistol didn't fire. Sparks flew from the frizzen but no powder ignited. The Cheyenne had once again dove to the side as he saw Ely point the pistol and then saw the sparks. He was as surprised as Ely when the pistol did not fire.

Once again, the warrior came to his feet facing the old trapper. He could now tell something was wrong. He raised the fist-sized stone club over his head ready to charge when a vicious growl shattered the stillness of the early morning as all of Jimbo's two hundred pounds hit him in the back and the big dog's powerful jaws clamped down on his raised arm.

The Cheyenne warrior fell face first and Ely could plainly hear the bones breaking in the warrior's arm as Jimbo bit down. The dog shook his head viciously, pulling the stunned Cheyenne away from Ely. Jimbo then released his grip on the arm and before Ely even realized what was happening, he bit down on the warrior's neck. Again, he heard bone being crushed as the huge dog bit down. The Cheyenne went limp, never to move again.

Jimbo wagged his tail as he came to Ely, who was stunned at the speed and viciousness of Jimbo's attack. He had known Zach since the very first Rendezvous and had known Jimbo since the second one. He had heard the stories others had told of the big dog and he had seen the aftermath of the dog saving Butterfly and her friend during that second Rendezvous, but this was the first time he had ever witnessed the dog actually attack. He reached down and patted the dogs head and asked, "Where did you come from boy? Is Grizzly Killer with ya?" Right then Ely was so amazed and relieved he wouldn't have been surprised if the dog would have answered him.

Ely kept working his hand as he watched the black sky slowly turning to the gray of early morning. As he rubbed his right hand and arm with his left, he softly talked to Jimbo asking, "Do ya think you could finish circlin' these here horses while I see if I can get my hand a workin'?" Jimbo looked up at him as if telling Ely just to show him. Ely pointed at the horses then moved his hand in a circle over his head, just like he'd seen Zach do countless times before and to his surprise the huge dog spun around and took off without making any sound at all.

Grub had made it a little more than half way around the horses when he saw another Cheyenne guarding the herd. By now most of the stars had faded from the eastern half of the sky, but the deep darkness was still hugging the ground. The guard wasn't moving, he was just sitting on his horse looking toward the gap. Grub figured he wanted to be at the gap where he thought the battle would be. It was obvious to Grub they were expecting to surprise the Shoshone with the ambush, expecting the Shoshone to just come riding through the gap.

Grub was fifty yards or maybe a little more from the guard as he watched the horses. It was hard to judge the distance in the twilight of early dawn but he knew he was within easy rifle range. Grub figured he would wait until he heard the first shot and then he would shoot from where he was hidden rather than chance stalking in close enough for a knife or tomahawk.

Spotted Elk would start the attack on the unsuspecting Cheyenne in the gap any minute now as the stars were all faded. Grub could now see the red ridge and the gap plainly. Suddenly without any warning he watched the Cheyenne guards horse rear up and the guard fall off the horse to the opposite side. The horse bolted away in fear and then Grub could see, what at first looked to be a very large wolf attacking the warrior. Only seconds later he recognized it was Jimbo.

The huge dog had approached from within the horse herd itself. The horses were all familiar with Jimbo and had made no fuss whatsoever. Jimbo had remained silent until he jumped, and his jaws clamped down on the Indian's leg just above his knee. The vicious growl and blinding pain caused such fear and shock in the Cheyenne Warrior and his horse that the horse bolted, leaving the shocked warrior on the ground. Jimbo released his grip on the leg as the Cheyenne fell but his powerful jaws clamped down on his face just a split second later.

Grub heard the muffled scream from the guard and could see his hands trying to push Jimbo away. He raced forward covering the fifty yards in only seconds, but it was all over when he arrived. As Grub raced up Jimbo stopped his attack. One of the warrior's eyes was out of the socket and resting on his check, his scalp was nearly torn off and there were tooth holes and torn flesh where only moments before had been a face. The Indian took in a gasp of air trying to hold on to life, but Grub knew he wouldn't live, and this would be a slow and very painful death. He reached down with his knife and put the Cheyenne out of his misery just as the first gunshot rang out from above the east side of the gap.

Jimbo took off toward the gap as Grub ran back toward where he and Ely had left the horses. Ely was already there. He was starting to get a little of the feeling back in his hand but he still couldn't make a fist. Grub noticed immediately something was wrong with his longtime partner. Ely's face showed confusion, and he was vigorously rubbing his hand and arm. They could hear now that the gap was fully engulfed in battle. The war cries of the warriors could be heard as the shots rang out.

With a concerned tone Grub asked, "What's a happened to ya, pard?"

"Don't know, I throwed my hawk at one of 'em guardin' the horses, and somethin' felt like it tore loose in my shoulder. It hurt like hell and then my hand went numb and I couldn't move my fingers." Grub watched as Ely worked his hand trying to make a fist. His fingers were now moving but just a little. Then Ely said, "They's startin' to wiggle a little now but I can't grip nothin'. My whole arm is tinglin' and now my hand is gettin' the pins and needles feelin'. What's strange is my shoulder hurt somethin' awful when I threw the hawk but now there ain't no pain in it at all; even that damnable ache is gone."

"I ain't sure we can, but we best mount up an' try to hold these here horses. If'n Spotted Elk and Grizzly Killer root out the rest of them there Cheyenne, they might try to scatter the herd as they leave."

Ely nodded and then they both stepped up into their saddles. As they did Ely asked, "Grub, did you see that big dog of Grizzly Killer's?"

"Yeah, just before I was ready to shoot the guard, he attacked. By the time I got there I just had to finish 'em off."

"He sure saved my bacon. My hawk just hit the guard in the arm and without my hand workin' I might a been layin' out there with my head bashed in if Jimbo hadn't a showed up."

They were both wondering how the big dog knew they needed him as they split up and headed to the same places around the herd where the Cheyenne Warriors had been holding the horses.

The shots above the gap were becoming more sporadic by the time Grub and Ely took their positions around the horses. Spotted Elk had climbed down to within just a few yards of one of the unsuspecting Cheyenne. He had waited until he was sure that all of the warriors with him were in position, then fired his 1803 Harpers Ferry rifle, hitting the Cheyenne in the back.

Zach had been sitting behind a boulder waiting for Spotted Elk when Jimbo had suddenly left his side. He knew his dog well enough to know he could sense something he himself could not and just watched him disappear into the darkness toward the horses.

Zach, Benny, Red Hawk, and Buffalo Heart had just fired their first shot when Jimbo appeared by Zach's side once again. He was behind the rock reloading when he saw Jimbo come running up to him. He could see the wet blood on the dogs face and knew there was at least one of the enemy they didn't have to fight.

The first volley of shots and arrows had been devastating to the Cheyenne; more than half of them had been killed or wounded. Zach was reloaded in less than a minute and brought his Hawken .54 up to his shoulder. He saw the gray powder hanging in the air seventy-five yards from him and waited for the Cheyenne to reload. Only moments later the painted face of the Cheyenne Dog Soldier appeared from behind a bush and Zach took aim as the Warrior brought his smooth bore trade rifle to his shoulder. Zach fired, hitting the Cheyenne in the face. The heavy lead ball going through and spaying two other warriors behind him with blood and gore.

Those two were the only ones Zach could see left alive on Zach's side of the gap and he yelled for the others to hold their fire. Only one more shot echoed through the gap from the other side, then all was quiet.

Although none of them spoke the Cheyenne tongue, they all understood the universal sign language and Zach signaled the two remaining Cheyenne to drop their weapons and come forward or die where they stood.

They looked at one another and dropped their bows, then Zach pulled his knife from his belt and shook his head. Both of them then pulled their knives and dropped them as well. He hadn't noticed but Jimbo wasn't by his side now and as the two young Warriors started slowly walking up the hill toward Zach, he heard Jimbo growl down the hill aways. Only a second later two more young Cheyenne warriors stood up backing away from the huge dog. Red Hawk started to laugh at the sight of Jimbo herding the four remaining Cheyenne up the hill toward Zach. Although Red Hawk wasn't laughing at the Warriors, one of them looked at him with a hatred in his eyes that made Zach shutter and wonder just where such deep-seated hatred between these tribes came from.

He had wondered many times after he had fought the Blackfeet, Cheyenne, and Arapaho, and even his first encounter with the Shoshone had been a violent one when several young warriors had stolen his horses and mules. What made the Indians so violent and what made them hate one another so vehemently? He could understand some of their hatred of the white men, after all the white men were strangers, coming into their land, killing their buffalo and trapping their beaver. Although some tribes like the Shoshone and Ute had, for the most part, accepted the arrival of the white trappers.

The hatred between the tribes was something different. It seemed that hatred went back to before the time of their grandfather's grandfathers. They were raised with that hatred, and although Zach had been successful in making peace between the Ute and Shoshone, he didn't see any way that was possible between the Shoshone and many of the surrounding tribes.

Fifteen minutes later, Zach and his group with their four prisoners met Spotted Elk who had seven of the Cheyenne with their hands bound on the bank of the creek at the south end of the gap. Only moments later Grub and then Ely rode up to them.

The Cheyenne were all young; Zach didn't believe the oldest of them was over twenty. He figured this group of young warriors was trying to make a name for themselves, earning the respect of many of the older warriors and probably the unmarried women of their village.

Spotted Elk learned through sign language that a young Dog Soldier by the name of Tall Bull had led this group and he had gone to three different Cheyenne villages recruiting warriors to make this raid. None of the older men in the villages would follow him and had told him he was foolish going that far from home so late in the year. Tall Bull was one of the Cheyenne that had been killed during the first volley of shots from the Shoshone.

Several of the Shoshone Warriors started driving stakes into the ground and Zach knew then these eleven young men were going to meet a very slow and painful death. Although he didn't understand the Indian way of dealing with their enemies, he knew it wasn't his place to interfere with it either.

About half of the Cheyenne were staked to the ground when Spotted Elk walked back to where Zach was standing with Grub, Ely, and Benny. Ely was still working and rubbing his hand, trying to get his fingers working. After greeting his brother-in-law, Zach said, "It might save many Shoshone lives in the future if you showed these Cheyenne you do not fear them by letting them go. Let them go back to their village and

33

tell everyone that the Great War Chief of the Shoshone has such strong medicine he does not have to torture his enemy, that he can kill them any time or any place, in his own land or on theirs."

Spotted Elk stared off into the distance and Zach could tell he was in deep thought. Spotted Elk and Zach both knew if he spared the lives of these Cheyenne that it would not be a popular decision among the young Shoshone Warriors that had followed him. Spotted Elk could see the wisdom in what Grizzly Killer had said if these young Cheyenne carried the word back to their villages it might make others not want to attack the Shoshone in the future.

Spotted Elk had matured into a truly great leader in the years Zach had known him. When Zach first met him in Willow Valley at the Rendezvous, he was like many of the hot-headed young Warriors following him now. Over the years and his many victories, he had learned the safety of all of the people was more important than revenge, counting coup, or the humiliation of their enemies.

He glanced back at Grizzly Killer and nodded but said nothing as he turned back toward where the Cheyenne were being staked to the ground. He said, "Release them." Several of the Shoshone looked at Spotted Elk like he was crazy, but Howling Dog was the only one that challenged the order, as he said, "We will not release them. We will make them pay for what they have done." Spotted Elk expected this response, but he stood firm, ready to force them to obey his order but also ready to explain to them the reason why.

When he was finished with his reasons most of the younger Shoshone was nodding their agreement. They could see the wisdom in Spotted Elk's decision but Howling Dog and his good friend High Back Bull stood alongside the Cheyenne they had just tied to the stakes unwilling to move. Spotted Elk stepped forward as Howling Dog shouted, "Is this the Shoshone talking or is the white of your brother speaking for you."

Zach stepped forward and High Back Bull stepped back but Howling Dog took his knife and dropped to his knees as if to cut the ropes holding the Cheyenne, but instead he slashed across the young Warriors belly opening him up in a gash over a foot long. There was fear, pain, and shock on the Cheyenne's face as Howling Dog defiantly stood facing both Grizzly Killer and Spotted Elk.

Zach started to step toward Howling Dog but Spotted Elk stopped him. He looked deep into the eyes of Howling Dog and said, "Do you want to be the War Chief of our people, Howling Dog?"

"If I were, I would not let the white man tell me how to fight our enemies."

"You believe I am wrong in letting our prisoners live."

"I know you are."

"All you need to do is kill me and then convince all of the Shoshone Warriors to follow you and you will be the War Chief."

Howling Dog started to look nervous as Spotted Elk handed Zach his rifle and stepped forward. He pulled his knife from its sheath, saying, "Howling Dog, I do not want to kill you, but I will. I will allow no man to ride with me that will not gladly follow my orders. You will never ride with me again, you will either die right here, right now, or you will leave now, but you will no longer be a Shoshone Warrior."

Everyone there knew the seriousness of the words Spotted Elk had just spoken. They all knew Howling Dog had gone too far. None of them knew just what the hot-headed young man would do.

Howling Dog's hand, holding his knife was shaking as the words slowly started to take effect. He knew he had just ruined his life unless he could defeat the older, more experienced War Chief. As Howling Dog stepped forward, High Back Bull ran in front of him, saying, "No, Howling Dog do not do this!" But Howling Dog brushed his friend aside and said, "I would rather be dead than let these Dog Soldiers go."

Red Hawk stepped forward, he had known Howling Dog his whole life and although they weren't real friends he said, "Howling Dog, what will you prove if you die here this morning? We just shared a great victory; do not let your anger make this be the last day of your life. Even if you win, no Shoshone will ever follow you into battle. Charging Bull will banish you from the village. Do not do this."

Zach could now see the doubt now in the young man's eyes. Spotted Elk remained silent but ready. He did not want to fight but if Howling Dog came at him, he would kill the young man and every Shoshone there, and Howling Dog knew it.

Several Moments passed in complete silence as everyone watched. Suddenly Howling stomped his foot, turned, and walked away.

Chapter 5

The Warriors Return

ZACH STOOD BACK as the Cheyenne Warriors were released. They all looked to be in their late teens and most had surprised and frightened looks on their painted faces. He knew well how deadly these young warriors could be and he hoped he was right that by letting them go it may prevent other battles with the Cheyenne in the future.

Using sign language, Spotted Elk told them, "Take your fallen Warriors and go back to your villages, tell your Chiefs never to come into the land of the Shoshone. I am Spotted Elk, the protector of our people, and I give you your lives this day, but I will not in the future. If you come into our land again, you will die the death of our enemy.

The Cheyenne, without any weapons, was still gathering the bodies of their dead as the Shoshone pushed their horse herd back through the muddy gap and started the eighty miles back to their village.

Only two of the Shoshone had been hurt in the fight and both wounds were minor. Spotted Elk knew their medicine had been strong today and as he rode along he thanked the one above for making their medicine stronger than their enemies. He like many of the Warriors that rode with him believed that with Grizzly Killer riding with them, his powerful medicine would strengthen their own and everyone knew his medicine was the strongest of all.

There was just a skiff of snow left in the shade of the short sage and rabbit brush as they headed west along the south side of the Sweetwater River. They weren't pushing the herd hard and Zach figured it would take them two full days to get back. The weather could be unpredictable in the Rockies, especially in the late fall. Today the sun was shining, but the air was still cold as they pushed further west.

Jimbo was out in front as usual with most of the Shoshone pushing the herd, keeping them bunched close together. Zach told Spotted Elk he would take Benny, Red Hawk, and Buffalo Heart on ahead and hunt. They would pick a site to camp for the night and hopefully have fresh meat for everyone when they got there. Spotted Elk nodded his approval, confident in his brother-in-law.

Grub and Ely rode along with Spotted Elk, leading the herd as they traveled through the valley of the Sweetwater. Ely continued working his shoulder, arm, and hand. By midmorning he was able to make a fist but the tingling in his arm and the pins and needles in his hand were still there. Although the tingling bothered him some, it was better than the continuous ache in his shoulder that he had lived with for most of the last year.

That ache in his shoulder had become like a constant weight he always had to carry. It slowed him down and had taken most of the joy from his life, but today it was gone. His shoulder and arm felt lighter, and it seemed to move easier than it had since the day he was shot. He carefully raised his hand up over his head and expected the sharp shooting pain would be there, but it was not. He noticed Grub was watching him and said, "My arm is still tinglin' some from throwin' my hawk this mornin', but that miserable ache in my shoulder ain't there." He held is hand out for Grub to see and made a fist, then said, "And even my fingers is startin' to work right again."

Grub smiled and said, "Ya know, Raven Wing told ya to keep workin' that shoulder. She said the more ya work it the better it would be."

"Ya I know, but workin' it always made it ache worse, but whatever tore loose in there when I throwed that hawk must a been causin' that ache cause it sure ain't there now."

Zach and Benny stayed together while Red Hawk and Buffalo Heart crossed to the north side of the river. Zach hoped to find a small herd of buffalo that hadn't started their migration yet, but he wasn't really expecting that. He figured at best they would be eating antelope tonight.

The valley of the Sweetwater is shallow and broad, and with no game in sight, Zach and Benny kept moving south away from the river. They were nearly three miles from the river when they came to some low hills on the far edge of the valley. They dismounted and crawled to the top, and to their surprise there were two herds of antelope and right in between them was a half dozen buffalo lazily grazing on the brown prairie grass.

A small wash separated the closest buffalo from the antelope but Zach couldn't tell if it was deep enough to conceal them if they tried to stalk in on the big humpback animals. Their only other option was to get back in the saddle and try an all-out run at the buffalo, but Zach figured they were too far away for that.

As good as fresh hump ribs sounded to him, he didn't believe they had a chance at taking one of the big beasts from where they were, so they would try to take a couple of the antelope instead.

Zach carefully took a piece of yellow trade cloth out that he carried for just this purpose and tied it the top of a sage. Antelope have exceptional sight, that being their best defense out here on the plains. Zach moved extremely slowly as he tied the bright cloth and very slowly let the branch of the bush back upright. Benny was watching the herd as Zach freed the cloth so it could flutter in the nearly constant prairie wind. Every one of the little prairie goats was looking directly at the little yellow flag and soon two young buck starting to walk toward them, curious as to what was fluttering in the wind.

Zach and Benny both had their rifles to their shoulders waiting for the two curious animals to get within range; Jimbo was motionless right by Zach's side. He had hunted these fast little antelope with Zach countless times and he knew to not even turn his head. Ten minutes passed, and it seemed like forever to the two of them knowing they couldn't move a muscle. Another ten passed and then another and still the curious but very leery animals kept their distance. After nearly an hour Zach's finger felt numb, he wasn't sure he would be able to pull the trigger when one of the young bucks started a slow trot toward them.

The small fast running antelope was getting close to being in range, Zach figured another ten or fifteen yards and he would shoot, when suddenly the sound of two shots rolled across the valley behind them. The young buck stopped, head up ears forward, every muscle tense as he stared forward. Without warning he turned and bolted away running toward the rest of his herd at the speed only another antelope can match.

All of the antelope then ran at top speed toward where the buffalo were and they too started to run. In less than a minute Zach and Benny were staring at a completely empty prairie. Disappointed Zach untied his yellow cloth and put it back in his pouch. As they stood up to walk back to where they left their mounts. Zach patted Jimbo on the head and said, "Guess I should a let you try to herd 'em to us feller." The big dog looked up at him with a look that said, "I tried to tell you that."

As they mounted up Benny said, "Maybe Red Hawk and Buffalo Heart had better luck."

"Hope so." Was Zach's only response.

They angled ahead toward the river once again and as they got close, they could see Red Hawk and Buffalo Heart each with an antelope over the back of their horses riding toward them. As they approached the brush and willows growing along the river, a doe and yearling buck whitetail deer bounded from the brush. Zach and Benny alike brought their rifles up and fired at exactly the same time and both fleeing animals dropped.

After gutting them, they tied them behind their saddles and the four men continued west along the river.

It was late afternoon when they figured they had gone as far as they should and at the next large horseshoe bend in the river was where they set up to camp. They had four fires burning with the deer and antelope roasting over each fire by the time Spotted Elk and the rest of them drove the horses through the narrow gap of the horseshoe bend.

Everyone was tired. It had been a long day, starting with nearly no sleep the night before and the early morning battle with the Cheyenne. The confrontation with Howling Dog had taken a toll on them as well. Seeing his friend leave had been especially hard on High Back Bull. He knew of Howling Dog's temper and knew he had been wrong in what he had done, but he was still his friend and it had been an exceptionally hard day on him. No one had seen any sign of Howling Dog since he had stomped away from them that morning.

The words of Spotted Elk that Howling Dog would never again be a Shoshone Warrior kept running through his mind, and High Back Bull wondered what would become of his friend. He had decided when they got back to the village he would talk to Charging Bull on Howling Dog's behalf and maybe save his friend from banishment from his own people.

The mournful howling of wolves could be heard not far from their camp as the moon appeared over the eastern horizon. The sky was clear and cold. Although it had been freezing every night for nearly a month now, Zach figured this was going to be the coldest night so far this winter. After they had eaten their fill of the fresh meat, most of them were sitting by the warmth of the fires with their buffalo robes wrapped around their shoulders.

There were some of the young warriors that still wanted to celebrate the great victory over the Cheyenne this morning and were dancing around one of the fires. Zach, Grub, Ely, and

Benny watched with smiles as the young men danced and then told of their greatness in the battle over and over again.

Zach wished Running Wolf was by his side; he was his oldest and best friend. No other man in the world except his father meant as much to him as Running Wolf did and at times like this he missed his friend. Jimbo raised his head and then rested it on Zach's leg as if trying to comfort him, knowing he was missing his partner.

When it was time for sleep, Zach rolled out his heavy buffalo robe next to the fire where he had been sitting and after setting two of the fire heated stones on the robe he laid down. This was the time he wished to be back in his warm teepee with his two beautiful wives by his side. He could imagine the feel of their warm naked bodies against his and that thought made it even harder for him to get to sleep.

By morning there was a half inch of frost on everything except the fires, and even the river was frozen over except out in the middle where the current was really swift. As Zach sat up and looked at the horses, there was a small layer of fog rising off their warm backs and their breath made it look like they were all breathing fire.

The air was indeed bitter cold, but it wasn't long until the fires were all built up once again. Zach looked across the fire at Grub and Ely and started to laugh. Grub, curious asked, "What so funny?"

"You two look like a couple of snowmen with your beards all covered with frost."

Ely then chuckled, and he said, "Lookin' at you, I reckon we do."

Grub watched Ely move and was amazed he actually seemed to be moving easier than he had since before he'd been shot and he asked, "Pard, how's that shoulder and hand of yours this mornin'?"

"It feels great, there ain't no tinglin' and that miserable ache is gone too." Grub smiled and shook his head, wondering just what Ely had done in throwing his Tomahawk that had helped his shoulder so much.

The deer and antelope carcasses were picked clean by the time they were mounted up and pushing the horses across the river to the north side. Another ten miles or so and they would leave the river heading northwest to where the Popo Agie and Wind River meet.

*****

Running Wolf stepped out of his warm teepee this cold frosty morning and looked toward the southeast, wondering where his partner was and if they had been successful. The cold air hit him like a knife as he breathed in and wondered how Grizzly Killer and the others had fared on this bitter cold night, knowing none of them had taken many supplies with them.

He turned and looked across the village, the frost had formed on the lower three or four feet of the lodges where the women had laced hides around the inside and stuffed grass behind the lining for protection from the cold. Above the frost line the tough buffalo hides used as the covering for the lodge poles was clear from the warmth of the fires within. The tops around the smoke flap was black from the constant fires that burned in the center of the lodges providing both warmth and light for the inside.

Running Wolf walked over to Grizzly Killers lodge to check on his sister, Sun Flower, and Little Dove and offered his help with anything they might need. Other than missing their husbands and not getting hardly any sleep they were fine. Little Dove had stayed with Sun Flower and Shining Star while their husbands were away.

Sun Flower had another miserable night. Her back ached, and the baby was restless, turning and kicking continuously. She had tossed and turned. Even with both Shining Star and Little Dove taking turns rubbing her back she could not get comfortable. She wondered how much worse it would get before this child of Grizzly Killer's would come out to meet its father.

Running Wolf went back inside his teepee and bundled up against the cold then saddled his chestnut gelding and rode out around the other horse herds. He stopped and talked to the young teenage boys that was guarding the herds. Although Running Wolf was Ute and very proud of his Ute heritage, he looked to everyone like a Shoshone. With his wife being Shoshone, it was her that fashioned his buckskins and he was dressed like Grizzly Killer and every other Shoshone man in the Village. After he had greeted the guards, he rode out nearly ten miles toward the Sweetwater, not really expecting to see Grizzly Killer and the others returning but hopeful just the same.

As he was riding back he killed a nice fat buck mule deer that was more interested in chasing a couple of does than he was about the man approaching on horseback. He rode back into the village and after cutting the deer up, he and Raven Wing took a large roast to Chief Charging Bull and another to White Feather and Bear Heart.

When they left her parents lodge, little Gray Wolf stayed with his grandparents. It was always a treat for Bear Heart to spend a little time alone with his grandson. Although he loved Star just as much, there was a special bond between grandfather and grandson.

It was late afternoon when one of the young men watching the village came running into camp shouting, "They have returned. They have returned." Everyone in the village stepped out of their lodges, and only a few minutes later they could see the nearly seventy horses and the men herding them triumphantly riding toward the village.

Chapter 6

Track of the Grizzly

A FEAST WAS PLANNED for the next day to celebrate their return and their great victory over the Cheyenne. A hunt was planned for the next morning; elk had been seen along the Wind River only ten miles north of the village. The only thing that put a damper on the festive mood was that Howling Dog had not returned. Charging Bull called for a council fire in his lodge where the chiefs and village elders would discuss the events that had happened. Howling Dog's father, Long Lance, had been a great warrior and was well respected in the village, but he, like everyone else, knew his son was short of temper and did not always see what was best for the people.

After the village elders were all seated around the small fire in their Chief's lodge. Charging Bull reverently removed his pipe from its highly decorated soft leather wrap and filled it with the mixture of leaves they used for tobacco. As the pipe was passed around the group, they believed their thoughts and prayers were carried on the smoke to the one above. After the pipe was returned to Charging Bull and had been put away, they all looked to Spotted Elk to find out what had happened.

Spotted Elk told them exactly what had happened. Some of them were angry at Howling Dog but others, like Long Lance, were sad that one of their own people had acted that way. There were questions asked of Spotted Elk about his decision to let the Cheyenne live but his explanation seemed to satisfy them all.

Long Lance had not said a word during the council and Charging Bull, like the others, could see the sadness in his face. Charging Bull asked, "My friend, it is a hard thing you have heard here. Is there anyone else you would like to hear from?"

The wrinkles around his eyes seemed deeper and more defined as he looked at Spotted Elk and then at Bear Heart and said, "Bear Heart, my old friend, I too take pride in your son. Spotted Elk has proven time and time again to be worthy of all of our respect. I, like the rest of you around this council, was once a great Warrior, and I had hoped my son would take my place as I have grown old. I believed Howling Dog would grow out of the anger, but it seems it has only gotten worse. I do not know why he is angry, perhaps I will never know. I would talk to his friend High Back Bull to see if he can tell us about this anger."

Spotted Elk left and only minutes later returned with High Back Bull. This was the first time High Back Bull had been invited to a council fire, and he understood its importance. After he was seated next to Spotted Elk, Long Lance asked, "High Back Bull, you have been a friend to Howling Dog, can you help us understand where the anger that has taken over his life has come from?"

Long Lance had never questioned any part of Spotted Elk's story; he believed Spotted Elk was a man of honor. He still hoped it wasn't too late for his son but he, like Spotted Elk, would not want a warrior riding with him he could not trust to do what was best for his people.

High Back Bull looked at the elders around the council, and then said, "I cannot speak what is in my friend's heart, but I believe he was jealous of Grizzly Killer and Spotted Elk both. He wanted to be greater than they are but did not want to wait until he could prove it. He wanted to be looked up to by all, and because everyone respected Grizzly Killer, Spotted Elk, and even the Ute, Running Wolf, and the other white men in the village, more than they did himself, he grew to hate them until that hate consumed him."

Charging Bull then asked, "Do you believe Spotted Elk did the right thing?"

High Back Bull looked at Spotted Elk, and shook his head as he said, "I believe Spotted Elk did what he believed to be right. But only time will tell if he made the right choice. I know what Howling Dog did was wrong and I know he would have fought Spotted Elk and died there with our enemies if it wasn't for the words spoken by Red Hawk."

"Do you believe Howling Dog will return to our lodge?" asked Long Lance.

"I do not know if time will heal his anger or if it will make it grow worse. I know Howling Dog has always been quick to anger, but I have never seen him like he was as he left us. If he returns, I think it will take much time."

Zach had sat in on many councils over the years since he had taken Sun Flower as his wife. This council had been only the village elders and chiefs except for the input from High Back Bull. Zach watched as the elders left Charging Bull's tent, he could see their mood was solemn. Although Long Lance was hopeful, he really didn't believe Howling Dog's pride would allow him to return.

It appeared to Zach as though Long Lance had aged during the meeting; his dark eyes seemed to be set deeper into the wrinkles around his eyes. Long Lance walked to the edge of the village. He needed to be alone for now. He felt, as well as looked, older after the council as he remembered back to when his son was just a boy. He was boastful and always in need of attention. He was given the name Howling Dog because he was so arrogant, always shouting about how great a warrior he was. Howling Dog had never learned that being a great warrior took much more than just shouting about one's greatness or even their prowess in battle. It took a deep commitment to protect the people.

Two large roasts from the buck Running Wolf had taken was on spits over the fire as Running Wolf and Zach looked over their horses. All of them seemed to be just fine even after the one hundred and fifty-mile journey to the muddy gap and back again.

Most of the snow had melted under the direct sunlight throughout the day, but the air remained cold and Zach could feel it getting colder the closer the sun moved toward the mountains just west of the village.

Zach thought about Howling Dog alone with no village or lodge for protection on this cold night. He knew Howling Dog could and would build a shelter and that he had the skills to survive, but Zach knew how hard it was to be by yourself through the long cold days and nights of winter in the Rockies. He had done it after his Pa had been killed, and if it hadn't been for Jimbo and Ol' Red, he wasn't sure he would have survived. He knew also that both of his animals were exceptional and he was extremely blessed that both of them were his friends.

He sat within the warmth of their outside fire as the flames roasted the fresh venison, watching his wives move about in and out of their lodge. He watched his friends and partner as they finished up their chores. He knew he would never feel alone again with these good people around him and he felt blessed to be here now in their presence. He watched Sun Flower with her huge belly struggle to reach down to pick up more firewood and he jumped up to do it for her. She smiled at him but shook her head and said, "It is my place, my husband. I do not wish you to do it for me."

Zach smiled at her but did it anyway and said, "It is your place to keep our child safe, my beautiful wife, and not over work yourself. She smiled and leaned into him, her small body almost like a child next to his large muscular frame. Zach leaned down and kissed her and thought as he had so many times before that he had to be the luckiest man in the mountains.

The air became bitter cold as the sun dropped behind the towering peaks of the Wind River Mountains. Shining Star and Raven Wing came out and started to slice off pieces of the venison to take back inside. Zach as well moved inside out of

48

the cold and took his place sitting on the hides that covered most of the floor of their teepee. Star walked toward him smiling and holding out her little arms, and as he picked her up, she said Papa. This wasn't the first time she had called him that, for the last couple of months she had been speaking a few words, but it still melted his heart every time she did.

Between the teepees of Zach, Running Wolf, and Benny, Zach's was the largest, and the women had all arranged for them to eat together. Soon Running Wolf, Benny, Ely, and Grub were sitting around the small fire in the center of the teepee. Raven Wing brought in a big black pot full of biscuits she had been cooking and Little Dove brought two large pots of coffee. They ate and talked and laughed in the dim warm light of the fire until they all were stuffed.

Each of them took turns telling Running Wolf about the battle with the Cheyenne. Sun Flower shuttered as she remembered her encounter with the Cheyenne. She and Raven Wing were taken and Shining Star nearly killed when a Cheyenne hunting party had stumbled onto their home on the banks of Black's Fork. As bad of a memory as that was for Sun Flower, it made her feel warm and loved inside because Grizzly Killer had come, just as she knew he would, and had rescued her, making the Cheyenne pay for what they had done with their lives.

Running Wolf hadn't wanted to stay behind but he knew what a great responsibility it had been to watch over and keep the women and children safe. Zach could see the longing in his eyes as Benny told of the battle and knew if anything like this ever came up again that he would be the one protecting their family while Running Wolf rode off to battle.

Ely told of him throwing his tomahawk and the pain and then numbness and tingling in his arm and hand and how it had taken many hours for the feeling to come back. Now he showed them all by making a fist that his fingers were working fine and the ache in his shoulder that had plagued him for much of the last year was gone, saying, "This here shoulder sure ain't like it was 'fore that ball tore through it but I don't reckon it's felt this good since that day." Raven Wing told him to keep moving it or it would stiffen up again.

Star fell asleep sitting on Zach's lap as the conversation died off around the fire. The men were all tired. They had ridden one hundred and fifty miles, fought a deadly battle against the Cheyenne and slept in the bitter cold all in the last three days. As the others all left Zach's warm teepee, Shining Star tucked Star into the warm bed of furs while Zach removed his buckskins. The warmth of the lodge felt good to him, but the real satisfaction was being back with his wives. Even though the three of them had been together for over five years now, he still marveled at the fact that these two very different women had become like sisters. He had decided long ago he would never understand why there was no jealousy between them. They never argued and truly seemed to love one another as much they loved him. He laid there on top of the large buffalo hide that was the bottom of their bed and watched the two of them put everything away and then slip off their soft doeskin dresses.

Zach never tired of watching these two beautiful women; he loved them both more than life itself. He watched Sun Flower, his first wife now with her belly extended so far it looked as if it might burst. He could tell she was physically uncomfortable, but she never complained. She had wanted for years to have Zach's baby and although her back ached all the time she just accepted her misery as part of her life and she had never been happier.

Zach could see that in her face, she had a glow about her even though he knew it was becoming harder and harder for her to do the daily chores. Shining Star was several inches taller than Sun Flower and she'd had a much easier time carrying Star. Sun Flower was a woman small in stature and the weight of the growing baby was sticking out in front of her so far it put a severe strain on her back.

As she laid down next to him, she rolled onto her back and Zach gently laid his large rough hand on her belly. He felt the baby move, and he bent down and kissed where he had felt the movement. In the position Sun Flower was laying, the weight of the baby was pressing against her and made it hard to breathe. Zach helped support her as she rolled onto her side as Shining Star laid down with them. Instead of lying next to Zach, she laid on the other side of Sun Flower and gently started rubbing her back. It wasn't long before she could hear Sun Flower's soft deep breathing and knew she had gone to sleep.

Shining Star then pulled the heavy warm grizzly robe up over them and carefully moved taking her place on the other side of Zach. She cuddled her warm naked body up to his, laying her head on his chest slowly running her fingers over his belly and beyond.

Jimbo was curled up between the door flap and Star, the big dog was never off duty. His job was to protect his family and the most helpless was the most important to protect and he took his job seriously. Whether they were on the trail or here in the village, he would defend his family with his life. Zach had spent the first winter after his Pa's death alone except for Ol' Red and Jimbo. He had spent most all of his time teaching them to obey his every command, but he had never had to teach the big dog to protect him or Sun Flower and Shining Star. Then, when Star was born it seemed he knew she was now his greatest responsibility.

Jimbo was even protective of Luna, Running Wolf's beautiful white wolf. He had saved her after a bear had killed her mother and siblings by chasing off the bear and had taken over the job of raising the tiny pup. As Luna grew she had become as protective of Gray Wolf and Star as Jimbo was. She usually stayed behind to protect her family whenever Running Wolf and Zach took Jimbo with them, whether hunting or trapping. No one had seemed to notice yet, but Luna was gaining weight rapidly as she was carrying Jimbo's puppies.

Jimbo had left Zach each morning since he had been a pup to go out on an early morning hunt. No rabbit, grouse, squirrel, ground hog or any small animal was safe when he and Luna hunted each morning. When Zach and Running Wolf was there, the big dog and wolf knew the family was safe and would leave for sometimes an hour or more on their morning hunts. If the men weren't there, they never left the area of the teepees.

The next morning Jimbo pushed his way through the door flap and whined softly outside Running Wolf's teepee. A moment later Luna pushed her way through the flap and the two of them disappeared into the darkness of the predawn cold. Although Luna was pure wolf, she was every bit as tame as Jimbo. She was large, weighing close to one hundred and twenty pounds, but as the two of them were together, she looked almost like a pup next the massive two hundred pounds of Jimbo.

As the morning dawned into a new day, the air was cold and crisp but the sky was clear and the slowly fading stars looked as though you could reach out and touch them. Red Hawk and Buffalo Heart stopped by to see if Zach or any of the rest of them wanted to go on the hunt this morning for the feast that was planned.

Even though Zach would have loved to go hunting, Sun Flower had started having pains a couple hour before and he would not leave. Running Wolf and Benny both rode out with the hunters, while Grub and Ely stayed in their warm lodge.

Raven Wing and Little Dove came to help if they could while Zach was pushed off to the side as a babysitter for Star and Gray Wolf. He could see his wife's face and although she was silent, he could see in her expression how much the pains hurt her as each one came and then left.

The sun was up and even though the air remained cold Zach could feel its warmth on his face as he carried the two toddlers across the village to the lodge of Bear Heart and White Feather. White Feather left immediately to go to her younger daughter and Zach stayed there with Bear Heart and the little ones.

It was nearly three hours before White Feather returned and told them it was a false alarm. The child of Grizzly Killer was not yet ready to meet its father. The pains had stopped and

Sun Flower was now resting comfortably. White Feather took Star from her father and told Zach they would keep their grandchildren for the rest of the day.

When Zach entered his teepee everyone but his wives left. Shining Star was gently rubbing Sun Flower back and didn't stop as Zach knelt down by them. Sun Flower smiled and said, "I think your little one wants to come and meet you Grizzly Killer, but it is not yet time." Zach bent down and kissed her then leaned over her to kiss Shining Star.

Sun Flower then said, "Mother told me, I cannot let this baby come before it is time, no matter how bad I wish it too. I have waited so long to give you a child, but I guess I have to wait a little longer."

It was a little after midday when the hunters returned with five elk being carried on eight pack horses. Running Wolf saw Zach watching them ride in and handed the lead rope of the pack horse he was leading to Benny then rode straight to Zach and with a worried look said, "My brother, on the way back not a mile from here we crossed the track of a big Grizzly." Zach stared out in that direction, knowing this could mean big danger to everyone in the village.

Chapter 7

The Bear Hunt

BY MIDAFTERNOON THERE was fresh elk roasting on more than a dozen fires. The remainder of the meat was being cut into strips for the drying racks. The sweet smell of the burning maple, chokecherry, wild plum, and cottonwood smoldering under the smoking racks soon filled the village and not long after the aroma of the roasting elk was making everyone's mouth water.

The elk hides had been staked to the ground and were being scraped when Zach saddled Ol' Red and rode out of the village to the place where Running Wolf had described the tracks of the big Grizzly could be found. The women working the hides knew they had to be fleshed before they froze tonight, or that job would be much more difficult tomorrow.

Zach urged his big mule into a trot as he followed the hunter's tracks north out of the village. Jimbo ran out in front of him and as he approached the area Running Wolf had described, Jimbo was already there sniffing the tracks as Zach slowed Ol' Red to a walk. There was no question this was a mighty big bear when he saw the tracks and dismounted to examine them closer. Jimbo was still and had a low growl coming from deep down in his chest.

The tracks were large, very large. In fact, Zach had only seen tracks this large once before in his life, and he figured they were made only this morning. The tracks were heading west toward the canyon where the Popo Agie runs out of the Wind River Mountains. Zach hoped the big bear was going up there to find a place for his long winters sleep, but as he looked at the tracks, he just didn't believe that is what the bear was doing. He unconsciously felt the claws of his famed necklace as the feeling of trouble came over him. Somehow he knew the big bear and himself would meet in the near future.

Zach was troubled as he rode Ol' Red back to the village. He wondered what the bear might do and why he was sure it was going to cause trouble. He really hoped he was wrong, but he didn't believe he was.

As he returned to the village, the sweet smell of the smoke from the fires under the drying racks mixed with the smell of roasting elk made his mouth water. That aroma was so enticing it made Zach even hungrier than he was before. He could not only hear his own belly growling but he could feel it as well.

It was still about an hour before the sun dropped behind the mountains to the west as he unsaddled and rubbed Ol' Red down with clumps of dry grass. He checked in on Sun Flower and Shining Star and found Sun Flower was now sitting up and feeling much better. He then headed to the teepee of Spotted Elk. After telling Spotted Elk of his feelings about the bear, the two of them went to Charging Bull. Both of these men took Zach seriously, neither questioning that he was right. They decided the horses were likely where the bear would strike if he indeed decided to do so. They doubled the guard around all three of the horse herds with Zach volunteering to take the last watch on the herd where is own horses were located. He was sure Running Wolf and Benny would fill in the earlier two watches.

Just as the sun disappeared behind the peaks of the Wind River Range, the roasting elk was ready. Sun Flower had been frustrated throughout the day as Shining Star and Raven Wing had been making and cooking biscuits so everyone in the village could have one at the feast tonight, but they wouldn't let her help at all. In fact, the only time they had let her get to her feet is when she had to go to the bushes and being pregnant made that need arise so often it seemed almost constant.

The village was indeed in a festive mood. A large fire had been built in the open area in front of Charging Bull's lodge. That is where most of the outside council fires were held. Zach helped Sun Flower to her feet and helped her dress for the cold as Shining Star got Star bundled up for the feast. Little Dove, Raven Wing, and Shining Star each carried their heavy black iron pots full of the fresh biscuits over to where others were cutting the succulent meat.

The air was cold, but that did not hinder the celebration at all. Zach carried Star with his right arm and walked hand in hand with Sun Flower. They could feel the heat from the fire as they sat down. Sun Flower wanted to serve Zach his supper but he would not let her. He made her stay sat down and take Star as he went to get both of their dinners, but he was turned away by Shining Star who soon brought them their food.

Many of the young people were already dancing around the big fire and the stories of their great victory was being told over and over again. Zach looked around at the people of the village, at the love they have of life and for one another and thought if more white people could see them like this, they wouldn't call them savages.

Zach thought about their trip to Saint Louis only a few months before and wondered what Emma and her husband, and even the banker, Mr. Chouteau, would think about this kind of celebration. He smiled to himself and thought, *"Why would I even wonder such a thing."* Zach loved his life living with these people, even though he did not always understand or agree with many of the things they did and believed. These were the most honest and loving people he had ever been around other than his own Ma and Pa. As he watched them chanting and dancing around the fire, he looked at Sun Flower who would soon have his child and then at Shining Star and Running Wolf, the love and respect he had for them was overwhelming. Although they were Ute from the other side of the great Uintah Mountains and had been raised as enemies of the Shoshone, they were now just as much a part of the village as Sun Flower, Raven Wing, and Little Dove were.

Star was watching as more and more started dancing around the fire. She smiled and pointed her fat little finger at them and laughed. Soon Red Hawk and Buffalo Heart came to get Zach, Running Wolf, and Benny to dance with them, so with Star laughing still in his arms, he too was dancing with the pounding beat of a rawhide drum around the fire.

They laughed, danced, and told stories of the victory over and over until fatigue and the cold started to drive them back into their lodges. The old was the first to go and then the young, and it wasn't long after the village was quiet once again.

Star was nearly asleep as Zach carried her into their warm teepee. Soon after, the toddler was fast asleep in her bed of soft tanned furs. It had been an enjoyable evening for all of them. Zach could see the fatigue in Sun Flower's eyes as she stripped off her warm coat made of coyote and wolf fur. She tried supporting her huge belly with her hands as she sat down on their bed and watched both Zach and Shining Star undress. She looked at Shining Stars naked body, with her small waist and wondered if she would again have the beautiful body that Shining Star had. It seemed to her that Shining Star had regained her shape after Star was born almost overnight. The baby kicked again and she smiled, thinking this child was going to be as strong as its father.

She knew women claimed to be able to tell whether the baby inside them was a boy or girl, but she had no idea which her little one would be. Since Shining Star had a girl she had hoped to give Grizzly Killer a son, but it really didn't matter to her. She had watched her husband many times as he played with Star and she knew he would love a girl just as much as he would a son. She knew it took over nine full moons before a baby was born and wondered just how much longer this little one would wait. She did not believe it was going to wait another two moons.

About four hours before dawn, Zach left his soft bed and the warm naked bodies of his wives and saddled Ol' Red and rode out to the horse herd. Running Wolf was on his chestnut and had just rode a complete circle around the herd when he saw Zach coming to relieve him. After telling Zach all had been quiet, he left to go back to his lodge and his warm bed next to Raven Wing.

Zach whistled Yankee Doodle Dandy softly as he rode around the herd; it was one of the very few songs he could remember from his childhood. Being raised on the frontier in Kentucky, he had never been around much music. Most of the time he just whistled notes he strung together, letting the horses know he was coming. Jimbo trotted back and forth in front of him, testing the air for any unfamiliar scent.

Zach didn't know how many times they had circled the herd as the early morning cold started to sink into his bones. He was watching the big dipper circle the north star and on clear nights like this, it was like looking at a clock to him. He knew it was only about an hour till dawn when suddenly Jimbo stopped. He pulled back on Ol' Red's reins and watched his big dog in the dim light of the stars. He couldn't see what Jimbo was looking at and didn't think Jimbo could see anything either or he would have taken off after it.

It seemed like he had been motionless for hours, even though it was only minutes. He watched his dog staring into the darkness, then Zach could hear the low soft growl starting deep down in his chest and watched the hair slowly rise down the center of Jimbo's back. Five minutes passed and then ten but Jimbo didn't move. Zach had carefully checked the powder in the pan of his .54 caliber Hawken and held it ready to fire.

Another ten minutes went by and Jimbo had stopped the low growling and the hair was laid back down along the ridge of his back. Whatever was out there, Zach knew was now gone. Was it the big bear? He may never know. Most the snow was now melted or frozen hard and the ground was frozen so there would be no tracks.

The stars had started to fade as the black sky above the eastern horizon was slowly turning gray, signaling the approaching dawn. Zach made another slow circle around the herd, stopping once again where Jimbo had caught the scent of something. He wished he knew what it was that had made his big dog growl. He was aware it could have been many things: a cougar, bobcat, wolf, coyote, or even a badger, but something was telling Zach it was the bear and that thought made him mighty uncomfortable.

Daylight came with no other troubles and the men on night watch all came into the warm fires as the younger herd tenders went out to watch over the herds during the day. Little Bull and Dull Lance where the two boys that came out to relieve Zach. Little Bull was 11 summers and Dull Lance was 13. The sun was still a half hour from rising as the two boys, bundled up in their warmest coats, greeted Zach. It was Dull Lance, trying to sound grown up that said, "Grizzly Killer, it is a good day, we will watch the horses now. You can go back to the warmth of your lodge."

Zach smiled at the two young men and said, "Yes, Dull Lance, it is a good day. The one above has blessed us with a clear sky and the rising sun promises us its warmth." Both boys smiled, feeling like they were grown up, relieving the great Grizzly Killer.

Zach stopped in his lodge only briefly, Star was still asleep but both his wives greeted him with big smiles. He could tell by the sparkle in Sun Flower's eyes that she felt much better today, and he was relieved. Raven Wing had told her to stay down and Shining Star was enforcing that by not letting her do any of the chores. So the only time she even stood up was for her frequent trips to the bushes.

Zach kissed both women then went to find Spotted Elk and Charging Bull once again. He told both men what had happened during the hour before dawn and he wasn't sure why he felt it was the bear but he did. Spotted Elk knelt down before Jimbo and gently rubbed the big dog's ears. The Indians are very superstitious, and they all believed the Great Medicine

Dog could talk to Grizzly Killer. They knew the dog couldn't speak words but Spotted Elk and Charging Bull alike believed if Grizzly Killer thought it was the bear, it was the Medicine Dog that was telling him that and they too believed it was the bear.

They called together the most experienced hunters in the village along with Grizzly Killer, Running Wolf, Benny, Grub, and Ely and planned to hunt the giant bear and remove the threat he posed to the village. Zach could see the disappointment on the faces of Red Hawk and Buffalo Heart for having to stay behind, but to their credit they did not complain. They both understood the importance of protecting the village while the hunters were away.

They started out from the horse herd where Jimbo had stood growling into the darkness with twelve men and four dogs. Jimbo was over twice as big as any of the other three dogs and when they got out some distance, he looked like an adult dog running with three puppies. Of the three other dogs, one was a couple years older the Jimbo and the other two were brothers and just a year younger. Just like Jimbo, they were all experienced hunters.

They were quite some distance from the horse herd when they could tell the dogs were on a scent. The warm rays of the sun was melting the surface of the ground and even though the scent did not appear to be strong, the dogs were following it fairly rapidly. At times it looked like they had lost the scent, but one of the dogs always seemed to find it again.

It appeared the dogs were heading toward the canyon of the Popo Agie and the rugged mountains beyond. As they got closer to the mouth of the canyon, the scent the dogs were following appeared to be getting stronger. They were running faster and didn't need to take any time finding the scent. The dogs were now moving faster than any of the horses could follow through the brush and trees along the river.

Zach had heard many dogs back home howling as they ran, chasing a coon, wildcat, or bear. These dogs, however, were not trained hounds, and the barking and howling was intermittent and to him completely inconclusive. As the dogs entered the mouth of the canyon, Zach caught just a glimpse of them and it appeared Jimbo was well out in front of the others. Zach had followed his huge dog on many hunts and Jimbo never did bark as he ran, making it harder to follow him. It seemed that the two younger dogs behind him were the ones being the most vocal. Otter knew his dogs, he could tell by the sounds the dogs were on a strong scent.

Once Zach and the others entered the canyon, the dogs could no longer be seen or heard so all they could do is try to follow their tracks. There was still snow under the pines on the south side of the steep canyon and that is where the tracks were leading, but the horses nor Ol' Red could climb the steep rugged hillside.

They left the horses and continued on foot. They hadn't gone even ten feet into the trees when the fresh track of the big Grizzly was plain for all of them to see. They stopped there to gather their thoughts and make a plan. They all knew then the dogs would not be able to tree the big bear, and they feared for the dogs. The four of them, even as big and powerful as Jimbo is, would be no match for a large grizzly and they all knew it.

Zach whistled just as loud as he could, several times, knowing if Jimbo could hear him he would return. Grub and Ely stopped right there and returned to where they had left the horses and built a fire. They were going to watch the horses while Zach and the rest of them continued up the steep snow covered hill. It took nearly an hour for them to fight their way out of the thick pines near the top of the ridge. Suddenly right before them was Jimbo, standing by Tracker, the older male dog. He was lying in snow stained red with his blood while Jimbo stood guard over him, licking his many wounds.

As they approached the two dogs, Tracker slowly stood up. Otter bent down as he slowly wagged his tail but he was weak from the loss of blood and he dropped to his knees as Otter touched him and he could feel his dog was trembling.

While Otter cared for his dog Zach and the others followed Jimbo another half mile to where the grizzly had stopped to face the dogs. Jimbo appeared to be unhurt, but it was only because of his speed. He had faced the big bears before and had barely been able to out run one of them. The two younger dogs had been killed with the first swipe of the bear's huge paw. Without any hesitation, the bear had caught the older dog as he tried to run, biting down through his hip. He would have died right there if Jimbo wouldn't have attacked the bear from behind. The grizzly released him and spun to attack Jimbo, but he was already a couple of jumps ahead. The bear came close to catching him but his speed saved both himself and the older dog, giving him time to get away.

Zach, Running Wolf, and Benny continued following the tracks of the bear with Zach now keeping Jimbo close to them. The tracks led over the ridge and down into another canyon that was so steep and rugged they could not follow through the slick snow covered rocks.

Zach stood there on the ridge top and followed the bear's tracks with his eyes until they disappeared around a ledge. He again hoped the grizzly would find a den for a long winters sleep, but the feeling he had was just the opposite, he felt confident the bear would be back to the village before he would den up for the winter.

Chapter 8

Missing Horses

LITTLE BULL AND DULL LANCE were still watching the horse herd as the sun passed the mid-way point in its daily journey toward the western horizon. Chief Charging Bull had been out to check on the boys earlier in the day. His encouragement was important as these two grew to be trusted warriors of their village. The Chief was proud of them and told them so; he like all of the village elders knew how important this younger generation of young men were to the future of their village.

Charging Bull thought about his old friend Long Lance and Howling Dog, his rebellious son. His heart ached for his friend and even though he had thought many times that Howling Dog was a troublemaker, he hated the thought of what may happen to him alone as the cold maker once again brought winter upon the land.

Red Hawk and Buffalo Heart had also been out and rode around the horse herds, checking on the young herd tenders. The boys all knew how important their jobs were and they took pride in doing it well.

*****

Meadowlark was sixteen summers old now and had caught Red Hawk's eye. She was pretty and had been secretly in love with Red Hawk since she was a child. As Red Hawk and Buffalo Heart rode back toward the village, they saw Meadowlark at the river filling buffalo bladder water pouches for her family. Red Hawk stopped, telling Buffalo Heart to go on ahead. Buffalo Heart laughed and told his friend, "Remember my friend, the dog chases the bear until the bear catches him. Don't get caught." Red Hawk hardly heard his friend; all he could see was the smile on Meadowlark's face as he dismounted and walked over to the river bank.

Basket Maker, Meadowlarks mother, was wondering what was taking her daughter so long to get water when she saw her and Red Hawk walking hand in hand back toward her lodge. She was ready to scold Meadowlark for taking so long but when she saw the reason she smiled, knowing that Red Hawk was one of the best young warriors in the village and her daughter could do no better. Within the small villages marriages usually happened with someone from another village so the blood lines did not get mixed, but occasionally they happened within the same village and it was not forbidden.

*****

It was near dark when the hunters finally returned. They had seen no other sign of the grizzly the rest of the day. Red Hawk and Buffalo Heart ran out the greet them and saw that Otter was carrying his dog in his arms. Both of them were sure Grizzly Killer would have taken the big bear and was mildly surprised to find out he hadn't. Jimbo ran up to greet the two of them and they both noticed the other dogs weren't with him. Otter called to them and they ran over and carefully took his dog as he dismounted. Running Wolf told them to take the dog to Raven Wing.

Raven Wing treated the dog's wounds, carefully working a poultice of healing plants into the deep holes from the bear's teeth. Jimbo stayed right there, gently licking the wounded dogs face as Raven Wing finished wrapping the wounds with strips of soft tanned leather. Otter was waiting outside with Running Wolf, Zach, Benny, Grub, and Ely. When Raven Wing stepped out, she told Otter to keep the dog warm and quiet. She then told him to try to get him to drink a fat rich broth, that he needed as much liquid and as much fat as he would eat to help replace the blood he had lost.

Even though Blue Fox, the old medicine man of the Shoshone, was still alive and it was he that had trained Raven Wing, his eyesight was now failing and nearly everyone was now going to Raven Wing as their healer. Her reputation as a Shaman and healer was growing all the time and many considered her medicine now stronger than that of Blue Fox. Everyone knew that come spring she would be leaving the village, and many hoped that time would never come. They believed their village was much stronger and better off with Raven Wing, Sun Flower, and their families living here.

Otter stepped inside and knelt down, gently petting Tracker, and then with Raven Wing's help they picked him up and took him to his lodge. Many in the village thought a dog was just an animal that you didn't treat as if they were a member of your family; after all, you may have to eat them. But to those that had gotten close to their dogs, like Zach, Running Wolf, and a few others, their dogs were a member of the family and they were treated just as good. Otter was a well-respected older warrior, and although some thought him foolish for caring for his dog that way, no one would ever say so.

As the sun dropped behind the western peaks, the cold started to settle once again on the village. Zach built up the fire outside his lodge and looked at the canyon of the Popo Agie. He wondered about the bear, where he was, and what he was going to do next.

Soon the aroma of cooking meat mixed with the sweet smell of wood smoke filled the air throughout the village. Once again Benny was bundled up, layered in a blanket Capote and a wolf skin coat that Little Dove had made for him. He walked by Zach with a greeting as he left to take the first watch of their herd.

Zach watched the two boys, Little Bull and Dull Lance, come back to the village. It had been a long day for them, from first light until dark. Both of them were exhausted but smiled and waved at Grizzly Killer as they headed for the warmth of their teepees.

Red Hawk and Buffalo Heart had made a teepee of their own. It wasn't as large as most of the teepees in the village but it gave the two young men a place out away from their families. Although they still usually ate their meals with their families, they slept and had all of their belongings in their own teepee.

Tonight Red Hawk took the first watch over one of the horse herds. Buffalo Heart was to relieve him when the big dipper had moved half way around the north star. Buffalo Heart overslept by a little and Red Hawk asked his friend, "Just what were you dreaming about that made you late?" Buffalo Heart apologized and with a sheepish grin as he shook his head.

Meadowlark had quietly left her parents lodge and had been waiting out in the cold for Red Hawk to return to his lodge. She was cold and almost ready to give up when he came riding in. He cared for his horse before entering his lodge then came right back out and got an armload of wood for the fire. She gave him enough time that she was sure he would be under the warm buffalo robe when she moved the entrance flap to his lodge and stepped into the warmth and light of his freshly built up fire.

Red Hawk was startled by the intrusion, throwing the robe off and picking up his knife. He was naked sitting there on the robe as she smiled and said, "You won't need your knife tonight," as she untied the laces on the shoulders of her dress and let it drop to the floor.

In the flickering light of the fire he could see the goose bumps on her cold skin. He watched her as she knelt down, put her hands on his shoulders and pushed him back down. He could feel her cold skin over the full length of him as she laid down next to him and he threw the robe up over them both. They made love for the first time through the early morning hours in the dim light of the teepee.

Red Hawk had never felt like this before and he was now sure this was the girl he would marry. She got up and added more wood to the fire and laid back down with him while the teepee once again warmed up. He watched her slowly put her dress back on; he had seen her and nearly every other girl in the village naked many times before. The boys and girls would often bath together and swim in the river when it was warm. He knew after tonight he would never be able to look at her again without remembering this night when she first gave herself to him.

Basket Maker heard her daughter carefully move the flap and enter their teepee but she didn't move or say anything. She smiled, knowing where her only daughter had been. She remembered back to when she was her daughter's age and had done the very same thing. She was glad her father was still asleep for he too would remember those nights when she had come to him and she wasn't sure that Wind in His Face would be as glad for his daughter as she was.

Daylight came and there had been no sign of the bear or any other trouble throughout the night. The younger boys once again took over their duties of watching the herds. No one knew it but Howling Dog had been watching the village and the horses from a distance. He was determined to make Spotted Elk and his white friends pay for what they had done.

Howling Dog blamed everyone but himself for being alone in the cold. He thought Spotted Elk had gone soft because of Grizzly Killer and the others. He believed all of the white men should be driven from the Shoshone lands or killed. He didn't care which but he had convinced himself it was the white trappers that were making the Shoshone cowards, afraid to torture and kill their enemies.

He was no fool, he knew that one man alone could not take on Spotted Elk, Grizzly Killer, and all the other warriors in the village. He knew that if he drove off the horses like the

Cheyenne had done the results would be the same for him as it had been for the Cheyenne. He watched the horse herd and didn't believe the village would keep up this day and night watch over them forever. When they quit the continuous watch he would sneak in and steal just a couple of the white men's horses each night. Before they knew they were missing he would be many days ride from here.

Howling Dog was satisfied with his plan as he watched the young boys relieve Grizzly Killer. He then watched Zach, riding his big red mule back to the village and wondered how a white man could have married two of the most beautiful women in all of the land. The more he thought about it the more the hatred he felt burned inside of him. He knew if he could get either one of his wives away from him that he would show them what a real Shoshone man was like.

Zach didn't unsaddle Ol' Red when he got back to his lodge. After checking on Sun Flower, Shining Star, and Star he mounted again and rode a large circle around not only the village but all three horse herds as well.

He didn't say anything to anyone, but he had the strange feeling someone or something was watching him ever since it had gotten light. He walked Ol' Red slowly, watching for any sign of the bear or anyone else. He paid very close attention to Jimbo, but he had not smelled anything to be alarmed about.

Howling Dog was still watching from a rise nearly two miles away. He knew the abilities of the Great Medicine Dog, at least by the stories that were told of him, so he made sure as he watched with the wind always in his face. He knew Grizzly Killer was looking for something as he made his slow ride around the village and horses, but he couldn't tell what that something was.

Three more weeks passed with not another sign of the bear and everyone now believed the big grizzly had found him a den for the winter. Although there had been other storms putting more snow in the high country, the snow was mostly gone in the valley and they moved the three horse herds together and moved them about a mile to better grass. Charging Bull declared the horses were safe and set only one guard on the large herd at night. The young men would still watch over the herd each day as a way to teach them responsibility. One guard would be posted and changed once a night; all the able men in the village would take a turn. That meant that only one night a month someone would lose a half night's sleep.

Meadowlark and Red Hawk were the only ones in the village that weren't happy with the news. Meadowlark had been with Red Hawk every night while Buffalo Heart was taking his turn with the horses and so they had kept it a secret from everyone except her mother and even Meadowlark did not know her mother knew.

It didn't take long for Buffalo Heart to figure out what was going on. He had spent almost every day of his life with Red Hawk and he knew him better than anyone. Red Hawk would disappear more and more during the day and soon curiosity got the best of Buffalo Heart and he followed his best friend. Red Hawk had made a wickiup in a thick stand of trees a few miles from camp. There he watched Meadowlark enter the wickiup and smiled but wondered why Red Hawk had kept this a secret from even his best friend.

That evening Buffalo Heart confronted Red Hawk, told him he had followed and wondered if he didn't trust his friend. Red Hawk felt bad. He trusted Buffalo Heart with his life, but he had made a promise to Meadowlark that he would not let anyone know about what they were doing.

Buffalo Heart could see how bad he had made Red Hawk feel and now they both felt bad. Red Hawk told him about the promise he made Meadowlark and he was so glad that his friend knew his secret. He now had someone he could talk to; it had been so hard for him not to be able to confide in his best friend. To tell him about the feelings he had for Meadowlark and how he planned to ask her father if he could marry her.

Buffalo Heart had mixed feelings about everything Red Hawk was now telling him. He was happy for his friend but at the same time jealous of him as well. There wasn't a girl in their village or anywhere else that he had met that he felt that way about. An awkward silence filled their lodge for a few moments then Buffalo Heart asked, "Does Wind in His Face or Basket Maker know of this?"

Red Hawk shook his head as Buffalo Heart said, "You better be careful. Wind in His Face is a great warrior and if he finds out before you tell him, it might not be good."

"I know but Meadowlark wants to wait," Red Hawk explained.

"Then I think you would be wise to keep your distance until you get his blessing," Buffalo Heart replied.

Red Hawk was silent and Buffalo Heart could tell he was in deep thought. Finally Red Hawk said, "I know you are right, but the way she makes me feel I just can't stay away."

"If you can't talk with her parents, you ought to talk to Charging Bull. You do not have to tell him what you have been doing, only that you want her and see what he has to say about it."

Red Hawk agreed that would be a good idea, but he'd promised Meadowlark he wouldn't tell anyone. As they crawled into their robes for the night, Red Hawk couldn't sleep, his mind troubled. He knew he loved Meadowlark, and he was happy when he was with her, but now he was miserable and didn't know what to do.

Morning finally came, and the village started to wake. The scent of burning pine became strong through the village as everyone warmed their teepees. Grizzly Killer, Running Wolf, and Benny saddled up and rode out to check on the horses but couldn't find several of them. Zach rode through the herd several times but the horses were gone. He had Benny go get Spotted Elk, Grub, and Ely, and it wasn't long before they were there as well. After going through the herd again Spotted Elk found he was missing horses as well.

Chapter 9

Scents of the Forest

HOWLING DOG HAD made several night time raids on the horse herd. He was proud of his ability to sneak in among the horses without disturbing them. He would softly whisper to them, stroking their legs and necks as he slowly led them away from the opposite side of the herd from where the lone guard stood watch.

Each night he had waited until the ground was frozen hard so there would be no tracks as he led the horses toward a timbered ravine with a small glade, well-hidden deep within the trees. The ravine was twenty miles to the southwest, near the pass that led up over the south end of the Wind River Mountains. He planned to take his herd of stolen horses over the pass to the Seeds-Kee-Dee, away from these Shoshone cowards that he had become ashamed of.

He had used dead fallen trees to form a corral around the glade where he would keep the horses until he had a sizeable herd. He would show Spotted Elk and all of his white friends what a real Shoshone warrior could do.

It was just after daylight when Howling Dog led three more of the stolen horses through the thick trees into the fenced off glade. He smiled at his success as he watched the fifteen horses happily grazing on the tall dry grass alongside the water

71

that slowly seeped from the ground forming a small pool and running just a few yards before once again disappearing into the soft ground. The water had a thin film of ice but there was enough movement of the cold water to keep it from freezing solid.

Howling Dog walked back into the trees where he had set up his small camp and stirred through the coals of his fire. Finding one small coal still hot, he carefully laid some dry bark he had rubbed in his hands, making it fray out and gently blew on the coal until it glowed and caught the bark on fire. He added small twigs until they caught and then large ones until he had a fire the size of his two hands.

He had taken a deer and had it hanging in a tree away from his camp, high enough it was protected from any predators. He went and lowered it enough to cut off a good-sized piece for him to roast.

*****

Zach and the others had carefully circled the herd, looking for any sign of which direction the missing horses would have wondered off. It was Ely that said, "These here horses didn't just wonder off, somebody took 'em." They all looked at him as he continued, "Why is it that only our horses is missin'? No-siree, them there horses was taken right out from under the guards noses."

Zach and Spotted Elk looked at one another and at the same time said, "Howling Dog."

It took nearly an hour before any sign was found of which way the stolen horses had gone and once again it was Ely that had found it. Grub shook his head as his old friend and partner called them to an area almost a quarter mile from the herd. Ely had found where some grass was bent over. Benny looked at the spot with a questioning look for there was grass bent over all around them. Even Zach and Spotted Elk wasn't sure why Ely believed this was the trail that the horses had used.

Grub smiled as he saw what Ely had found, both of them waited to see if any of the others would see. After a couple of minutes, Grub finally said, "Boys, what this here partner of mine is tryin' to show is a trail plain enough to follow if'n ya know what yer lookin' at. See how this here grass is bent over like all the other grass around here," they all nodded and then Spotted Elk saw it too. There was another just a step away bent in the same direction, and then another after that still bent in that same direction. The trail was so subtle that even after Ely had pointed it out Benny had a hard time believing it was really a trail.

Zach had Jimbo sniffing all around but where the horse herd had been all around this area, the scent was just of the herd. Zach thought maybe Jimbo could follow once they got further away from the herd.

The trail was not easy to follow, Howling Dog had not led the stolen horses in a straight line and he had taken a different route each night. Even Ely's sharp eyes would lose the trail and again they would have to back track to the last place he was sure he was on it and go from there.

Even as upset and angry as Spotted Elk was, that one of their own would do such a thing, he admired the skill that it had taken Howling Dog to hide his trail this well, and he was convinced it was Howling Dog that they were following.

By midday they were not over five miles from the herd. All they knew for sure is the trail was leading them in a southwesterly direction, but there were literally hundreds of places before them that a dozen or two horses could be hidden. The only choice they had was to continue to follow the trail.

As the Sun dropped behind the peaks to the west, Ely marked the trail with two rocks stacked one on the other and they rode back to the village. It had been a long frustrating day as they had tried to follow the faint trail left by Howling Dog and the stolen horses. They all believed they would find their horses and Howling Dog but Zach truly wished Howling Dog would just leave. He did not want to see him killed, but he was sure that is what Shoshone justice would require.

They had decided as they rode back to the village that they would put two more guards on the herd tonight but they would stay hidden. If Howling Dog came again to take more horses, he would be seen. Once again Zach volunteered to take the last watch of the night.

As he entered the teepee, he could see a distressed look on Sun Flower's beautiful face as she tried to smile up at him. Shining Star was preparing their meal and caught their little girl as she went running to her father as he knelt down beside Sun Flower. Star squealed her displeasure as Shining Star picked her up not wanting her to trip and fall into Sun Flower.

Sun Flower had had a particularly rough day. The ache in her back would not ease at all, and she could not make herself comfortable no matter how she tried to lay. The pressure the baby was now putting on her was nearly unbearable. There was no more room inside for anything but the baby and she had to go the bushes to relieve herself so often she wondered if lying back down was even worth it. Not only did her belly now look like was going to split open, it felt like it as well.

White Feather had just left when Zach had gotten there after spending much of the day with her daughter. None of them believed the baby would wait much longer before it came to meet his father. Although none of them knew for sure, they believed it was a boy simply because of how big the baby seemed to be.

To Sun Flower it seemed like she would never be comfortable again, or she would never get another full night's sleep. She hated the fact that she kept both Grizzly Killer and Shining Star awake with her frequent trips to the bushes. Shining Star felt sorry for Sun Flower; her own pregnancy had been so much easier than what Sun Flower was going through. She and Raven Wing had talked but not in front of their sister. Both of them were worried that with Sun Flowers small body and the baby being so large she may have a terribly hard time giving birth.

With almost no sleep at all Zach bundled up to go out and relieve Running Wolf from watching the horses. Since it was mostly their horses that had been taken, Benny, Running Wolf, and Zach had decided they would split the watch. Although known only to Spotted Elk and Charging Bull, Red Hawk and Buffalo Heart joined Spotted Elk and set another watch further out away from the herd. They kept to the shadows and still for the whole night, hoping they would see the horse thief before he reached the herd.

As daylight broke and the boys came out to take over the watch, Zach saw his brother-in-law and two friends walking toward the village. He smiled figuring the three of them had been out there all night long.

Zach was pleasantly surprised that Howling Dog, if it was him, had not tried for more horses this night. He knew it would have meant a fight and if Howling Dog would have been killed, it might have caused hard feelings among his friends and family.

When he got back to his lodge, Raven Wing and White Feather was there tending to Sun Flower while Shining Star was watching the two toddlers and preparing their morning meal. Sun Flower looked up and smiled at him as he stepped through the opening but he could see through the smile how miserable she really was.

She hadn't been able to stand up without help for a couple of weeks now, but now she even needed support to relieve herself. Raven Wing was worried about her sister although she hadn't said anything to Zach. He could tell by the look in her eyes how worried she really was. White Feather looked up Zach and said, "This little one of yours is a stubborn one. I think he waits a little too long to meet you."

Just then Sun Flower moaned and they all could see a contraction rake across her abdomen. Her mother and sister both turned back to her and White Feather said, "I do not think it will be long now my daughter."

Zach took Star over to Running Wolf's lodge so she could play with Gray Wolf as he paced around the outside fire worried about his wife. It was about an hour later that Shining Star came out and told him to take Star and Gray Wolf to

Butterfly so they could play with their cousins and for him to take the men and go find the horses. That he was just making them all nervous with his pacing.

Shining Star could see the worry and concern in his face and said, "My husband, Sun Flower has all the help she needs, it would be better for her and all of us if we didn't have to worry about you as well." Zach opened his mouth to protest, but she held up her hand to stop him. She then turned to her brother and said, "Running Wolf, take Grizzly Killer and go find the horses. You men will be of no help here for now." She smiled at both of them, knowing how her statement had sounded, but she stood firm and pointed at the mountains peaks reaching for the sky just west of them.

Even though none of them, except Grub and Ely, had much sleep, they all saddled up and headed to the stones that marked where they had left the trail the evening before. Zach had hunted and followed game ever since he was barely old enough to follow his Pa. He considered himself a good tracker, but as he watched Ely follow the scant sign, he just shook his head in amazement. He had never seen anyone he thought was as good at tracking as Ely Tucker and said so. Grub nodded his agreement and said, "Yes sir, theys just ain't none better than that there partner of mine when it comes to trackin', man or beast." Even Spotted Elk nodded his agreement that Ely was the best he had ever seen.

Zach's mind wasn't on the trail that Ely kept them on as the hours past. He couldn't get his mind off what was happening in his lodge. Was Sun Flower alright? Running Wolf kept a close watch on him and Jimbo as well. He knew his partner wanted to be back in the village but he also knew the women didn't need or want him in their way. He remembered back when Raven Wing gave birth to Gray Wolf and how she had bled. He had been sick with worry, but now, just as then, the men could do nothing about it. Giving birth was for the women to do and the women to help. It was men's duty to stay out of their way. He smiled knowing how much easier that was to say than to do.

By late afternoon Ely was on the ground, pointing to the timbered ravine that he believed the tracks where leading to. Zach stood in his stirrups and looked ahead. No more than half a mile in front of them, movement caught his eye. As he watched, one of his pack horses walked out of a brush lined gully and into the open.

He alerted the others, but they were too low to see the horse and they all wondered if that gully is where they were all being held. Staying out of sight, they spit up and approached the lone horse from both north and south. The horse seemed glad to be back with the others and whinnied when she caught the familiar smell of her friends. Running Wolf got down and checked her over and could see no injuries at all. They all wondered what had happened that she had been left out here alone.

It was a mile from where they stood to where the ravine opened up onto the valley floor. They left the mare there grazing, mounted up and started at a slow walk toward the dark timber filled ravine.

As they approached, the hair down the center of Jimbo's back started to raise and Zach could feel the muscles start to tense in Ol' Red. Buffalo Heart's gelding started to shy away from the dark trees and Ely motioned for them all to dismount. They ground picketed their mounts and continued to the edge of the trees on foot.

It was about a half mile through the dark timber to where the glade opened up and as they got ready to enter the trees Ely stopped and pointed to the ground. The tracks showed several horses had ran at full speed out of the trees and a couple of them slipping in the softer soil at the edge. They all studied the ground closely but none of them could find a reason the horses would have been running that fast.

An eagle cried out high overhead and out in the valley of the Popo Agie, the distant croaking call of a crow could be heard, but the dark pines were eerily silent. Zach could smell the musky order of earth and rotting logs, he could smell the pleasant scent of pine and spruce, but there were no squirrels barking their dislike of the intruders to their forest nor the cry of the blue jays. There were no woodpeckers hammering into the bark of the many pines looking for a meal and they all knew from this eerie silence something was wrong.

Chapter 10

The Dream

CONTRACTIONS HIT SUN FLOWER every few minutes for over two hours, but then they stopped. As bad as they hurt, she had wanted them to continue. She wanted to have this baby, Grizzly Killer's baby, that she had waited all these years to have, but the contractions had stopped. She was weak and tired; it had seemed like forever since she had been able to sleep. Every time she started to dose off she would again have to go relieve herself.

She wore a crystal tied to a rawhide string around her neck that she had ever since she had first felt ill from the pregnancy. The crystal was a beautiful piece of quartz with gold threads running through it. It had come from a hill in the Uintah Mountains west of their home on Black's Fork.

Zach had found gold nuggets in the creek below the vein of quartz from where the crystal had been found. Raven Wing and the others believed the crystal to be a healing stone, and ever since Sun Flower had first felt the effects of morning sickness on the trip to Saint Louis, she had worn the crystal. She caressed the stone, hoping its power would help her give Grizzly Killer a healthy child.

*****

Ely was still following the tracks of the horses as they pushed their way into the thick forest. It was dark under the canopy of pine and spruce; the sun had now disappeared behind the towering peaks and dark heavy storm clouds were covering the sky.

Jimbo was only a few feet in front of Ely and Zach and as he stopped, so did everyone else. Zach could see every muscle in the big dog was tense and the hair once again started to stand up down the center of his back. They couldn't see more than a few yards in front of them through the dark timber and what light was left was fading fast.

Everyone was tense and silent, not a sound could be heard, and even the breeze from the fast-moving clouds was not penetrating the thick forest. A blinding light flashed right in front of them followed immediately by the ear splitting clap of thunder. The ground trembled as the thunder shook them, making the forest around them tremble as well.

Zach, like the others, was momentarily blinded by the brilliance of the flash of lightning, but in the brief moment before his eyes had reacted to the flash he thought he saw the shape of a huge bear standing before them. Instinctively he cocked his rifle, but when he could see again, there was nothing there. Jimbo hadn't moved, the hair still standing down the center of his back. No one else said anything about seeing something in front of them and Zach wondered whether he had really seen a bear or if it was just his imagination. Another bolt of lightning hit the hillside above them followed by more ground shaking thunder.

The light was now gone in the forest. Ely knew he could still follow the track in the soft pine needle floor under these trees, but nothing about this felt right to him. He looked at Zach and then at Spotted Elk and shook his head saying, "I figure we best pick up this here trail in the mornin', we done lost what little light we had and I expect we is gonna be gettin' wet 'fore we get back." Zach nodded; there was definitely a look of relief on the faces of the others. A chill ran down the back of Running

Wolf and he wasn't sure whether it was from the cold or the feeling that something was wrong. Not wanting to turn their backs on whatever was making them uncomfortable they all slowly backed until they were out of the forest.

Once out of the trees there was still some light, it was then they turned and jogged back to their horses. Ol' Red was bigger than all of the Indian ponies. His long ears stood well above all the others but every one of them had their ears erect facing the ravine.

Snowflakes were starting to fall as another bolt of lightning flashed, this time more than a mile north of them. Zach could still feel, as well as hear the thunder as it rolled across the valley directly east of the Wind River Mountains.

Zach figured they were twenty miles from the village and he too was relieved to be out of the dark forest. With the wind to their backs they urged their mounts into an easy lope and headed back to the village, picking up the one horse they had found as they went.

Zach thought about his wife. He was excited to have another child, but he felt bad that Sun Flower was having such a hard time. He remembered back when Raven Wing had given birth and how frightened they had all been for her because she had lost so much blood, and they'd had such a hard time stopping the bleeding. He thought about how small Sun Flower is and her tiny waist that was now expanded to an enormous belly and he wondered how a baby that big would ever fit through her small hips to come into this world. He remembered Shining Star and how much easier the birth of Star had been, but Shining Star is a larger women than Sun Flower.

The snow was coming down hard and it was pitch dark as the riders saw the first light from the fires of the village. Zach had worried all the way back and was in a near panic as he jumped off Ol' Red. Running Wolf took the reins of the big mule and Zach just nodded his appreciation then ran to the teepee entrance.

He threw the flap to the teepee open and stepped through. He was in such a rush he startled the four women and both children that were sitting around the fire eating. Sun Flower smiled up at her husband and asked, "Are you in a hurry my husband?" All four women giggled at the expression on his face and Star held out her fat little arms for him to pick her up.

Zach breathed a deep sigh of relief as he saw Sun Flower was alright. In fact, she looked better than she had in several days. Her eyes sparkled with the light from the small fire and cast a rose colored tone to her cheeks.

He looked around at the other women who were all staring at him and finally smiled and said, "I was just worried about my wife." Then little Star would not be ignored any longer and squealed, demanding he pick her up.

As Zach reached down to pick up Star, Raven Wing and Little Dove got to their feet to leave for their own lodges to care for their husbands. A moment later they both came back in with their black pots, getting some of the stew they had made for their husbands.

As Zach sat down cross legged in front of the fire, Shining Star handed him a bowl and filled it full of the thick rich stew. There was both elk and deer, camas and yarrow root, along with cattail shoots. It had been on the fire simmering for hours and the water had thickened into a rich gravy. He reached for a biscuit that was still in the heavy cast frying pan and just dropped it on top of the stew. His mouth was watering as he took the first bite and smiled at the tender meat and succulent flavor.

Other than the frequent trips to the bushes, Sun Flower had a more restful night than she had in the past week. Both Zach and Shining Star needed the rest nearly as much as Sun Flower did. Zach could feel the baby moving inside of her as she cuddled next to him and wondered whether he would have another daughter or a son. Everyone seemed to think it was going to be a boy, and they thought that is what he would want, but it truly didn't matter to him. He knew he could not love any child more than he did Star and another girl was just fine with him.

As he dosed off, he dreamed of the new addition to his family, but one time he was dreaming of holding a baby girl and the next time it would be a baby boy. He had thought many times, especially over the last month, what the name of the new baby would be and in his dream when he was holding the baby as a boy he would call him Jack after his own Pa, and when he was holding the new baby as a girl she was called, Little Moon.

He awoke surprised to find everyone still asleep for the dream had seemed so real. He thought about the names, he liked the idea of a boy named after his own Pa, but his Pa's real name was John like his father before him, but he'd always been called Jack or Captain Jack by others. Zach thought about that and decided if it was a boy his name would be Jack Connors. He had clearly called the little girl in his dream Little Moon and as he laid there and thought about it, he had no idea at all where that name had come from.

Zach was awakened by Sun Flower and helped her get up. He helped her out into the cold dark night to relieve herself again. The fast-moving storm had left only an inch of snow in its path and already the sky was clearing. A few stars were shining through the breaks in the clouds and then a small crescent moon showed itself between the fast-moving clouds. Sun Flower shivered from the cold and wrapped the warm buffalo rode around her even tighter, then looked up at the moon and said, "It is good to see you little moon." Zach didn't say anything to her as they ducked back inside the warm lodge, but as he laid back down, he thought about the moon again and knew it would be a mighty good name for the baby as well.

Morning came, and Sun Flower felt much more rested and said, "Grizzly Killer, go find our horses today. You need not worry about me, Shining Star. Raven Wing, my mother, and all the other women in the village are here if the little one decides this is the day.

The sky was clear of the passing storm as Zach stepped out into the early morning light. Running Wolf and Benny had already saddled all of their mounts. Luna was with Jimbo and for the first time Zach noticed she had gained weight and commented that maybe she should go with us and run some of the fat off. Running Wolf called her over and rubbing her ears he said, "I think she has the same fat problem as Sun Flower, I believe Jimbo is gonna be a daddy too."

Running Wolf never said a word to Luna, but she licked his hand and then went over to the flap of their lodge and sat on her haunches, standing guard while Jimbo and the men were away. Zach watched the pure white wolf and grinned, wondering what the puppies would be like.

The sun was just cresting over the eastern horizon as Spotted Elk, Red Hawk, and Buffalo Heart joined Zach, Running Wolf, Benny, Grub, and Ely. Charging Bull came out to wish them well. He was still upset and sad that one of his people, the son of an old friend, had turned against his own.

Charging Bull knew that none of the men riding with Spotted Elk today wanted harm to come to Howling Dog but he was sure that if Howling Dog fought them, they would do what they had to in order to recover the horses that had been taken. He prayed that the one above will make Howling Dog find the right path for he did not want to have to tell his friend Long Lance that his son had been killed.

Meadowlark was standing outside her parents lodge watching Red Hawk as they rode away from the village. She wanted to go to him before they left but knew she couldn't. Red Hawk watched her as well, but he wasn't the only one; every one of the riders as well as Charging Bull had seen the way the two looked at one another.

Charging Bull smiled. He, like her mother, Basket Maker, thought the two of them were a good match. He could tell they didn't want anyone to know the way they felt, but he didn't understand why. He thought both Wind in His Face and Basket Maker would be pleased to have their daughter with a young man like Red Hawk. He watched Meadowlark step back inside with what he thought was a look of sadness. Then he walked along the stream to a small clearing about a quarter mile from the village where he could be alone and pray for the wisdom he knew he must have to guide his people through the difficulties he felt sure were coming.

Jimbo took the lead just as he always did, but instead of Zach being in front, it was Ely. Zach really didn't know if there was an Indian in the village that could track as well as Ely, but he was convinced neither he nor anyone in this group could. After watching Ely follow the scant trail the day before no one questioned him, they stayed back out of his way and let him lead.

When they came to the gully where they found the lone horse, they abandoned the line they were following to the timbered ravine and followed the gully south. They had gone over a mile when they saw, between large clumps of oak brush and stunted aspens, another six of their horses. Continuing on another half mile they found three more. These horses seemed content grazing in this gully so they turned back to the west heading for the dark timber and hopefully where Howling Dog had the rest of the horses held.

None of the seven of them were excited to enter the eerie darkness of the timber filled ravine. Zach and Benny were probably the least superstitious of any of them but even they weren't comfortable going back into the timber, not knowing what they would find. The fleeting image of a large grizzly once again flashed through Zach's mind, and as they dismounted he felt compelled to tell the others what he might have seen.

Even though the light was cut way back as they entered the trees, the bright sun and clear blue sky still let plenty of light down to the forest floor. They hadn't gone more than ten yards into the thick trees when a squirrel ran up a large spruce and out onto a branch, chattering his dislike of the intruders. Another step and a blue jay flew from a tree squawking his warning as he flew. These were the everyday sounds of the forest and hearing them made them all relax somewhat, but by the time they were a hundred yards into the thick forest it was quiet once again. No more squirrels, jays, or any other sign of life could be found and all of them felt anxious once again.

Another hundred yards and they could see light through the trees ahead. A few more steps and they all knew they were approaching an opening in the trees. Ely motioned for everyone to spread out and be quiet and they slowly and quietly approached the glade. First, they saw the dead fallen logs that Howling Dog had used for his corral, but there was no movement at all. Zach had spread out and was on the far left end still back in the trees away from the glade. He could see a small clearing just ahead. Two more careful steps and he could see the ring of stone used for a fire and knew someone had been camping there.

He waited and listened but there was no sound. Jimbo was only a step in front of him and the hair was once again standing up down the center of the big dogs back. Zach could no longer see Running Wolf or Benny. Even though they were the closest to him, the timber was too thick. He took another step, watching where he placed his foot, and then another. Now he could see a buffalo sleeping robe on the ground. The deep low growl started from way down deep in Jimbo's chest as Zach stepped into the small clearing that Howling Dog had used for his camp. Howling Dog's bow was lying on the ground and then he saw drag marks in the soft forest floor leading out the far side of the small clearing. He was looking all around but the thick trees were hiding anything that was there. Then, Ely's voice broke the silence as he said aloud, a single word, "Damn."

Chapter 11

Killing Just For Fun

SUN FLOWER LAID on the buffalo robes watching Star play, she loved her as if she was her own. She felt the child inside of her kick and move and wondered to herself if she would feel any different about the child she was carrying than she did about Star; after all they both were Grizzly Killer's. She had watched Shining Star suckle the growing child, wondering how much longer she would need her mother's milk.

She watched Shining Star heating their leftover stew for their morning meal, and she was so grateful for her at this time. Sun Flower smiled at her beautiful sister as she remembered back to the Ute village. It was on Rock Creek on the south side of the Uintah Mountains when she and Grizzly Killer had first met Running Wolf's sister. She and Shining Star both felt they were meant to be with Grizzly Killer and had ever since that first meeting. She remembered how torn their husband had been about taking a second wife although neither she nor Shining Star had ever quite understood why.

She was sure that the one above had guided both of them to him, for if he hadn't, she did not believe she would love Shining Star as her sister, just like she loved Raven Wing. They heard voices outside of the warm teepee, and Sun Flower smiled, recognizing the familiar voices of her mother and sister. Star rushed to her grandmother as she entered the lodge and then to Gray Wolf as Raven Wing almost dropped the squirming boy as he struggled out of her arms.

They were all concerned about Sun Flower. If the size of her belly indicated the size of the child she was carrying, none of them could see how, being so small in stature, she would be able to deliver the baby. Sun Flower was the only one that wasn't worried about it. She had dreamed of the future many times and always she was with Grizzly Killer and Shining Star as they watched their children play. She did not believe she would have had these dreams if the one above did not intend her to raise Grizzly Killer's child.

*****

Zach stopped, waiting for Ely to continue, a minute passed and then another, as they waited for Ely to speak again. It was Grub that spoke next, "What is it pard? What ya got over there anyhow?" Zach still couldn't see any of the others through the dense trees, but then Ely answered, his voice even louder and sounding more concerned than before, "Watch yerselves boys. We gots us a half dozen dead horses here, and only a mighty big bear could a tore 'em up like they is."

Zach heard a sound to his right and jumped, bringing his Hawken to his shoulder as Running Wolf stepped from behind a tree. He shook his head and smiled at his partner then shouted to everyone, "Best pair up. Nobody should be in these thick trees alone if'n there's a Grizzly in here with us."

Zach waited until Running Wolf was by his side then pointed out the drag marks in the small clearing. Two more steps and both of them could see the huge bear tracks and dark blood that had soaked into the soft ground.

They continued on out of the little clearing and into the thick trees, following the drag marks, afraid of what they were going to find. Jimbo was no more than a step ahead of Zach and Running Wolf when he stopped. Zach could now see there was an open glade just a few yards ahead, and he caught the movement of Grub walking toward Ely through the trees. Both he and Running Wolf were looking all around, their rifles up and ready to fire, but they could see nothing but trees all around them. Jimbo wasn't moving and Zach knew that something, either the body of Howling Dog or the bear was very near.

The hair on Jimbo's back was still on end, and Zach could see the big dog's nose testing the air all around. Zach and Running Wolf had taken on grizzlies before. In fact Ol' Red still carried the scars from a huge bear that had killed some Shoshone hunters clear down where Lost Creek runs into Weber's River. It was a few days travel west of their home on Black's Fork. A quick glance between the two of them and they both knew neither of them wanted to face another grizzly.

Jimbo started forward again, moving very slowly and as Zach followed, Running Wolf had to step behind him because of the thickness of the trees. Three more steps and Zach stopped. He could see a bloody leg sticking out of a pine thicket just a few feet in front of his big dog.

He could now hear the deep growl once again as it softly started from deep in Jimbo's chest. He was motionless, all but his head as both he and Running Wolf continued to scan the forest all around them. Another step and Running Wolf too could see the leg. Zach stopped and motioned for Running Wolf to watch as he bent down to pull the body from the thicket.

Just as Zach reached toward the leg, Buffalo Heart's voice not far to his right sounded, asking "Grizzly Killer, are you over here?" The voice had startled him just as he was about to put his hand on the leg and he jumped making Running Wolf tense up and take a deep breath himself. Zach softly spoke to his young friend saying, "Yeah, right over here, we've found a body." Zach could hear Buffalo Heart and Red Hawk coming through the trees toward them as he reached forward and grabbed the leg to pull the body from the thicket.

Zach pulled but there was very little weight, the leg and been gnawed off just above the knee and just a section of shattered bone is all that came from under the low pine boughs.

Buffalo Heart had just stepped around the last tree and saw the leg just as Zach pulled it into the open and stopped dead in his tracks at the gruesome sight.

They all started looking around but they could see no other parts of the body. They were still only guessing that it was Howling Dog, although they believed he was the only one that would have tried this, none of them knew for sure.

They were now only ten feet from the edge of the glade and Zach urged Jimbo forward as the four of them made their way to the opening. Ely was stooped over, studying the ground as Grub watched the tree line for any movement from behind his partner while Spotted Elk watched from forty yards away.

Ely stood as Zach and the others approached, and then he motioned Spotted Elk over as well. The hair down Jimbo's back was still standing on end as he started sniffing the tracks that Ely had been studying.

Zach looked at Spotted Elk and said, "I found where he was camped and then between there and here we found a man's leg, chewed off just above the knee. There is no tellin' how far the bear could have carried the rest of him."

A sadness showed on Spotted Elk's face as he asked, "Is it Howling Dog?"

"I couldn't tell; the moccasin and leggins were gone," was Zach's response but everyone there believed it could be no one else.

Ely spoke, "It appears the Ol' Bruin was just killin' for the fun of it. None of these here horses has been ate on much. He must a figured the man was a better meal than the horses and took him with him to save the rest for later." A shutter ran down Red Hawk's back as he thought of being eaten by a bear and hoped Howling Dog was already dead when that happened.

Ely showed them where the bear had attacked the horses from and figured there must have been a good breeze blowing in the bear's face or he wouldn't have gotten that close before the horses spooked. The grass around the seep and across the glade had been torn up by the panicking horses as they tried to escape the attacking bear. When they finally broke through the logs that Howling Dog had used to contain them it had been too late for the six that were lying here in the glade.

Grub said, to no one in particular, "This is a bad one boys, this Ol' Grizz should be sleepin' in his den by now and he ain't, and now he has a taste for man. Nobody in the village is gonna be safe if'n we don't find 'em.'"

Spotted Elk nodded his agreement but added, "How many of us is he gonna kill when we do?" He then looked at all of them and continued, "When the sun rises tomorrow, we will divide all of our warriors. Half to protect the village and with the rest we will track the great bear." They all nodded as they headed back into the timber and out of the ravine. They all waited in the glade as Red Hawk and Buffalo Heart went back into the trees and wrapped the leg in Buffalo Hearts coat. They were taking it back to the village for a proper burial.

As they cleared the trees and headed out to where they had left the horses, Zach and then Jimbo stopped and looked back. Zach rubbed his dog's ears and said, "I know boy, I feel it too." Running Wolf was watching him with a questioning look and Zach said, "He's up there; I can feel him watching us." At that they all stopped and looked back, not one of them doubted that Grizzly Killer and his Great Medicine Dog could feel the bear's presence.

They mounted up and swung back to the south and the gully where the surviving horses had finally stopped their panicked run. The nine horses didn't seem to mind joining them as they headed them back to the protection of the herd.

It was late afternoon when they had the stolen horses safely back with the herd and had made their way into the village. Nearly everyone there, stepped out of their lodges to meet the returning men. Long Lance was standing by Charging Bull as Spotted Elk, Zach, and the others rode up to them.

Long Lance could see by the expression on their faces that they had found his son. He knew whatever had happened was brought about by Howling Dog and not these men before him, but that knowledge did not make losing his son any easier. His head was down looking at the ground as he listened.

Spotted Elk spoke, "We found the horses and part of a body, it is only a leg and we cannot tell who the leg belongs to." Long Lance looked up, now with the question he had plainly showing on his face. Spotted Elk continued, "The great bear. It appeared to have found them sometime during the night. He killed six of our horses and the man that was holding them, but all we could find was this leg the bear left behind."

Charging Bull didn't speak, he was thinking about what he had just heard would mean to his people, but Long Lance asked, "May I see the leg?" Red Hawk and Buffalo Heart rode forward and reverently laid the leg still wrapped, on the ground before Long Lance. When they carefully unwrapped it, a collective gasp arose from the village and Long Lance just stared at the torn and bloody leg. He like everyone else believed this was his son but from this ripped up leg there was no way to tell for sure.

Charging Bull put his hand on his friend's shoulder, as Long Lance said, "This was not a good way for any man to die." They all nodded their agreement as Red Hawk looked up at Long Lance and his Chief. Charging Bull nodded, and he carefully rewrapped the leg.

Howling Dog's mother had died several years before and Long Lance had taken another wife. Although she had tried, Howling Dog had never accepted her as family and Long Lance believed his mother's dying was one of the reasons Howling Dog always seemed to be so angry.

Buffalo Woman had made Long Lance a good wife, but she never understood the anger and hatred that Howling Dog always seemed to have toward her. She loved Long Lance every bit as much as she had loved Standing Bear, her husband of many years that had been gored by a buffalo during a fall hunt. Because of her love for his father, she had never stopped trying to become a part of Howling Dog's life.

Buffalo Woman came to her husband's side then bent down and picked up the wrapped leg. She turned toward the stream where she would wash and prepare the leg for burial. Though none of them knew for sure, the leg would be buried as though it was Howling Dog's whole body. They all knew that this would help Long Lance, believing his son was buried as a Shoshone Warrior.

While Buffalo Woman was preparing the leg, several other women erected a small teepee and built a fire directly in front of the door. When Buffalo Woman was satisfied that the leg was ready for burial, she set Buffalo Heart's coat aside and wrapped the leg in an elk hide that she had tanned to make rabbit fur lined leggings for Long Lance for the winter. She knew this hide would mean more to her husband used this way.

She brought the leg to the newly erected teepee and laid it on the ground as if it was the complete body of an honored Shoshone Warrior, lying in state before the burial. She sat down opposite the leg to watch over the body, as someone always did until it was covered with rocks, earth, or laid in a cave or cavern.

Long Lance was the first to enter, then he too sat down next to his wife. Next to enter was Charging Bull, showing his respect not for the hot-headed and arrogant young man, but to his old friend Long Lance. By the time all light had faded from the western sky everyone in the village had stopped by, showing the respect they all had for the village elder and the sadness they felt for his loss. As Spotted Elk turned to leave, Long Lance stood and held his arm out and the two of them clasped hand to arm. This was Long Lance's way of telling Spotted Elk that he had done the right thing for the village.

Finally, High Back Bull entered and sat down on the other side of Buffalo Woman and said, "Howling Dog was my friend. May I have the honor of sitting with him through the night?" Long Lance looked at the young man and then Buffalo Woman. She gave him a slight nod. He looked back at High Back Bull and nodded. He struggled to his feet and then helped Buffalo Woman to her feet. When they stepped outside of the small teepee, they were both surprised to see Charging Bull, Spotted Elk, Red Hawk, and Buffalo Heart sitting around the outside fire, keeping it burning so the fallen warrior's spirit could follow the smoke into the dark sky and find the Milky Way to lead him to the other side. Long Lance sat down with them, showing his appreciation for their support.

Once again Charging Bull saw the way Meadowlark and Red Hawk looked at one another from afar and wondered how long the two young lovers would try to hide their feelings for each other.

Zach went out after dark with Jimbo and slowly rode Ol' Red around the horse herd one more time. He was hoping the bear would stay back in the timber now that he had plenty to eat but checking just the same. On the far side of the herd, Jimbo stopped and Zach watched the hair start to rise down his back once again. That made him think about what Ely had said about the bear killing just for the fun of it and that had made him worry all the more.

Zach stared out into the dark but only a minute later the hair on Jimbo's back laid down, making him wonder if the man killing bear was out there or Jimbo had just caught an old scent.

Chapter 12

On the Lake's Edge

AFTER CARING FOR Ol' Red, Zach stepped back into the warmth of his teepee to the smiling faces of his two beautiful wives and playful little girl. This had been a good day for Sun Flower. although the baby had been very active, she had not had any serious pains and other than her frequent trips to the bushes, she had been fairly comfortable all day.

After kissing Shining Star, Zach sat down next to Sun Flower and leaned over to kiss her just as little Star came running to her father. Their lips barely touched as Star jumped onto Zach's lap. They all smiled as Star threw her little arms around him.

After Star had gone to sleep for the night, Zach laid down next to Sun Flower while Shining Star finished her chores. Zach put his hand gently on Sun Flowers extended belly and smiled as he felt the baby move. He remembered back to the first time he had ever seen her at the warm springs by the Bear River. In his mind he could still see her there, naked in the warm water along with Raven Wing and Butterfly. It had always amazed him how she could parade around naked in front of others and not be the least bit shy or bashful about it.

Sun Flower was watching his face, wondering what he was thinking and finally asked, "What is my husband thinking of?"

95

Zach replied, "I was remembering the girl I met at the warm spring's years ago, and how beautiful she was. Now that girl is my wife and even more beautiful than she was then." Sun Flower's eyes sparkled at his words even though she knew her huge belly wasn't attractive. However during all of this long pregnancy, Zach and Shining Star had always made her feel as though she was.

Shining Star slipped her soft tanned doeskin dress off and laid down with them. Zach was between these two beautiful women and as they both cuddled up next to him he thought once again, as he had so many times before, *"I am the luckiest man in the mountains."*

A strong gusty wind started blowing in the night and by the time the morning fires were started, the stars were all hidden by a heavy cloud cover. No snow had fallen but there was no doubt in anyone's mind that snow was coming.

Charging Bull had a large fire started in front of his lodge and sent word for every warrior in the village to gather. When Zach, Running Wolf, Benny, Grub and Ely arrived, the village elders were already seated around the fire. They, like all of the warriors, gathered in a circle just outside of the seated Elders. Spotted Elk was seated next to Charging Bull and Bear Heart, his father next to him. Long Lance was seated on the other side of Charging Bull along with Otter.

Charging Bull unwrapped his ceremonial pipe and each of the elders prayed for the safety of their village and hunters, letting the smoke from the sacred pipe carry their prayers to the one above.

After the pipe was returned to its ornately decorated wrapping, Spotted Elk and Charging Bull divided the warriors into the groups, one that would protect the village and the other to track the bear.

Not everyone in the village knew of Ely's skill at tracking and was surprised when Spotted Elk told them that the hunters would follow Ely. He let them all know how dangerous hunting the big bear will be and it would take the very best of each one of them to find the bear before he kills again. Some seemed angry or hurt that they would have to follow a white man, believing their own skill at tracking would be superior to that of his. Charging Bull stood and spoke to the hunters that expressed those feelings, "Ely, has been a trusted friend of the Shoshone for many years and his skill at following a trail has been proven many times, but his eyes are not the only ones that will be hunting this great bear. It will take the best of each one of you to keep our village safe." Everyone nodded their agreement and Zach smiled at Charging Bull's ability to know exactly what to say to appease the egos, especially of the very proud younger men.

As the hunters prepared to leave for the hunt, they took jerky and some pemmican along with their sleeping robes. None of them knew where the great bear would lead them and with the storm coming in they all prepared to be gone for several days.

Zach did not want to leave Sun Flower as she could have the baby at any time. Even though the women assured him there was nothing he could do, he would not leave. He, like many of the others staying behind to protect the village, wanted to go, but he knew his place was with his wives at this time.

Just before they rode out, Long Lance came to Spotted Elk and asked him if he would take the leg of his son and bury it with the horses he had stolen. That the spirits of the dead horses may carry his spirit across the Milky Way to the land beyond. Spotted Elk solemnly nodded and assured Long Lance his son would be given a Shoshone burial.

Raven Wing and Little Dove watched their men ride away. They knew both were great hunters and warriors, but both women would have felt better if Grizzly Killer and his Great Medicine Dog would have been riding with them.

Not long after the hunters had gone, heading toward the thick timber in the ravine, a half dozen warriors along with the boys that normally watched the herd headed out, relieving the guards that had been there the last half of the night.

Zach was politely driven from his teepee as Raven Wing, Little Dove, and White Feather all arrived. White Feather smiled at her tall blue-eyed son-in-law and said, "You and the Great Medicine Dog go and protect the village, we will care for my daughter." She then smiled at him, letting him know she appreciated the way he cared for her daughter. White Feather knew how deeply Grizzly Killer loved her daughter and that Sun Flower could not have found a better man. She also thought of Shining Star as another daughter and Star was every bit as much her grandchild as was Gray Wolf. White Feather loved her daughters being here and was grateful that Grizzly Killer and Running Wolf had stayed here for Sun Flower to give birth. She, like everyone else in the village, believed the village was stronger with her daughters and their great husbands here.

Zach saddled Ol' Red then patted Jimbo's head and said, "Well feller's, looks like we got kicked out, let's go see what other trouble we can get ourselves into." Luna was just outside the teepee staring at the mountains west of them. Zach was sure the white wolf knew right where Running Wolf was whether she was with him or not. Zach believed this wolf really was Running Wolf's spirit helper and had been even before Jimbo had found her.

Luna's belly had been growing even faster than Sun Flower's and as Zach reached down the run his hand down her beautiful white fur, he figured she would be having her and Jimbo's puppies any day now as well. He spoke gently to her, "Do you want to go with us as we check around the village, pretty girl?" She looked up at him and licked his hand, then put her paw on the teepee as though telling him she must stay to protect the women and children in the teepee. Zach nodded to her and rubbed her ears one more time. Then, with Jimbo ahead of him, he headed out.

He went north along the Wind River for over five miles, riding in and out of the brush. He was looking for any sign the big Grizzly had been this way. He carefully watched in the mud along the water's edge and for any place the ice along the edges that might have been broken. When he turned to head back, he had not seen anything and Jimbo's nose hadn't picked up any dangerous scents either.

Zach looked at the mountains to his west, and marveled at their beauty, but his thoughts took him back to Black's Fork, the place he had considered his home for the last five years. It had been over six months since he had been there and he missed looking out across the big meadow at his and Running Wolf's small horse herd. He missed the familiar sight of the towering peaks of the Uintah as they reached for the sky.

He then looked again toward the dark timber of the ravine where he knew Running Wolf and most of his friends were looking for the killer bear. That thought brought him out of the memories of Black's Fork and back to the present. He knew there was no better tracker in the land than Ely Tucker and there were enough of them they could stop the killer grizzly, but still he worried. Zach had faced enough of the big bears to know just how hard they were to kill.

He rode around the village once and then again, noting there were at least a dozen other warriors and Chief Charging Bull all actively watching.

*****

Ely lead the group of hunters through the dark timber into the glade where the six horses lay forever still. Once again they were on foot, having left their own mounts a full half mile from the mouth of the ravine. They had not tied them so they could graze and run if the bear came at them as well.

Ely, like the rest of them, had no idea where the big bear would have taken the rest of Howling Dog's body. He asked the others to bury the leg while he searched the area where Grizzly Killer had found it. It took him only minutes to find a trail he knew he could follow.

The leg was placed at the base of a large pine and covered with rocks. Rocks were not plentiful in the thick forest, even with all of them working it took over a half hour to adequately cover the leg so predators could not get to it.

99

Ely was hoping the bear would stay close to be able to feed on the dead horses but there was no sign the grizzly had been in this area since his original attack. Ely had found the trail where the bear had carried the rest of the body away. There were some blood drops and an occasional drag mark. While the others were burying the leg, Ely followed the trail for a ways through the thick forest before turning back.

Once Spotted Elk was satisfied with the burial, they spread out and started up the ravine behind Ely. Within a half mile of the glade the ravine started to narrow and another quarter mile it was nothing more than a steep rocky gorge. The bear had continued going up, Spotted Elk made the comment that at least he was heading away from the village and all nodded knowing that was a good thing.

Running Wolf was carrying Zach's .54 caliber Hawkin. Zach had insisted he take the heavier rifle, leaving Zach, Running Wolf's .50 Caliber. Zach had purchased the .54 right from the Hawken's Brothers gun shop when they were in Saint Louis earlier this year. He had carried the .50 caliber ever since he had won it in a shooting contest at the very first Rendezvous over five years ago. Although both were fine rifles, Zach figured the heavier .54 caliber ball would be a little better at stopping the big grizzly and he wanted his partner to have all the advantage he could against the man killing bear.

It was plain to see the bear was still carrying the body; there were bloody drag marks now as the grizzly climbed over the rocks. Some of the rocks were large enough the men had to use both hands and feet to climb up and over them. Running Wolf was on the north end of the men. Through the forest he hadn't been able to see Ely and Grub at the center but now the trees had thinned out and he was quite a bit higher than they were in the bottom.

Running Wolf was now high enough up the side of the gorge he could see a fair distance ahead of them. It appeared that the top of the gorge opened up again into a basin not more than a mile ahead. He could also look back down over the tops of the trees and the hidden glade and out onto the valley floor.

He could see their horses peacefully grazing and all the way back to where the village was located not far from where the Popo Agie runs into the Wind River. The distance was too far to see the actual village but the smoke haze was plainly visible showing him the exact location.

It took them another hour to make the hard steep climb up to where the gorge finally opened up into a basin. Although this was the first time Running Wolf, Benny, Grub, and Ely had been here, Spotted Elk and some of the others had hunted this basin in the past. It was not a regular hunting area however because it was so hard to get to.

They regrouped once they were out of the gorge and Otter, who was the oldest of the Shoshone, told of a small lake at the upper end of the basin. He went on telling how the lake was surrounded on three sides by sheer rock cliffs and if the bear was using this area as his home, the lake was his only source of water.

With Ely staying on the trail the grizzly had left, the others once again spread out. The cloud cover was lowering; now the peaks and higher mountain tops were hidden by a thickening layer of dark gray clouds. A snow flake landed on Running Wolf's face as he watched well out in front them. They all believed there must be cave or den the bear was using.

Spotted Elk was next to Ely on the south and Grub next to him on the north as they pushed westward, closer to the lake. With over a dozen men moving toward the water, they believed the bear would run rather than fight if they were to push him out of his den.

The bottom of the basin was not level and there were small washes and patches of heavy brush. Some brush and undergrowth was so thick it was hard for them to push through. Ely stayed with the bear's trail, at times on his hands and knees, wondering how a bear this big got through some of the brush. He found more than just a little of the grizzly's hair on the brush as he crawled through it and the hair confirmed it was a silver tipped grizzly they were tracking.

The snow had started to fall but only lightly and an hour later they climbed up over a natural dam, and there sat the lake before them. All of their eyes focused on the same thing sitting at the water's edge, the mangled remains of a mostly eaten man.

Chapter 13

The Birth

BY LATE AFTERNOON Zach had ridden around the village a dozen times, ranging out as far as three or four miles along the streams. With each completed circle he would check on Sun Flower only to be sent away once again.

He had found a small knoll just north of the Popo Agie where he could sit and watch both north and south with a pretty good view. The knoll was about two miles from the village which was close enough that he knew if it became the baby's time, someone would let him know. He had made sure Charging Bull knew where he would be. Charging Bull used the knoll himself quite frequently for his early morning prayers and thought not only was it a good vantage point but it was also a spiritual place where the one above would answer his prayers. He let Grizzly Killer know that as he rode Ol' Red out of camp.

When he reached the knoll, Jimbo was already at the top of it waiting for him and Ol' Red. Zach stepped out of his saddle and loosened the cinch a little and just let the big mule graze freely, knowing he would not wander far.

With Running Wolf's Hawken in his right hand and a buffalo robe in his left, he climbed the seventy-five yards to the top where Jimbo was anxiously waiting. He dropped the robe and moved his hand in a circle over his head. That was the signal Jimbo was waiting for, the silent hand signal telling him to scout a large circle around the knoll.

As Jimbo took off, it still amazed Zach how a dog that big could move so fast and still not make any noise. He figured, just like he had learned in the thick woods of Kentucky just how to set his feet down without making any noise, Jimbo had learned that with his feet as well, but the dog had four of them. He watched the big dog disappear into the brush then he sat down, pulling the buffalo robe around his shoulders. He faced west toward the setting sun, but with the thickening dark clouds he could only imagine where the sun might be. The top half of the Wind River Mountains was now locked away within the approaching storm and Zach wondered just where Running Wolf and the others were by now. Had they found where the bear had gone? Were they caught up in the snow yet? Were they all safe? He wished he was there with them, but then the thought struck him; this must be what Sun Flower and Shining Star go through every time he is away, and it made him wonder how they delt with it so well.

Jimbo returned from his scout and with a wag of his tail told Zach all was clear. As the light faded earlier than usual because of the heavy cloud cover, Zach could no longer see out across the valley to make his vantage point usable. Before he left the top of the knoll, he looked up into the clouds and asked God to protect his friends this night. He then bowed his head, closed his eyes and thanked God for this life he was living and for the unparalleled beauty around him. He prayed for the safety of Sun Flower and the baby and the safety of everyone in the village.

A Wolf howled in the distance between him and the mountains and a moment later he heard Luna answer the call. He wondered for a moment if they could understand one another, then he smiled at himself and said right out loud, "Course they can." However, he thought it was unusual for the wolves to be howling on such a dark and dreary night and he wondered what they knew that he didn't.

The light was almost gone as he unsaddled Ol' Red and rubbed him down with a clump of dry grass. The mule shook and threw his head up and down when Zach had finished. That was the mule's way of saying thank you to the man he had spent nearly every day of his life with.

As Zach stepped inside the teepee, all of the women except White Feather were still there. White Feather had left to go prepare the evening meal for Bear Heart. The women had prepared a stew with the last of the fresh elk and thickened it with a little flour. Then like they had learned in Saint Louis, they made biscuits but instead of cooking them in a pan they sat them on top of the stew and put coals over the lid so they would bake. The camas and cattail shoots they had gathered before everything had frozen would not last them more than a couple of more weeks and then their diet would be mostly meat, supplemented with pemmican for the rest of the winter.

After being out in the cold all day, Zach enjoyed the warm stew and the warmth of the teepee. The wind was gusting some and Shining Star gave the wooden bowl she was using to feed Star to Little Dove while she stepped out into the cold to adjust the smoke flap to better draw smoke from the small fire inside the teepee. It took only a moment and the air inside cleared considerably.

Zach watched Sun Flower's face. Although she hadn't said a word he could tell something was wrong. He looked to Raven Wing, and she too had seen the expression change on her sister's face.

Suddenly Sun Flower dropped the wooden bowl, the thick hot liquid landing on her bare lower leg. It burned her skin, but she didn't seem to notice. Zach was on his feet along with Raven Wing. They got to her just as Shining Star stepped back inside. Star cried for her mother but Little Dove held the little girl then got Gray Wolf as well.

Shining Star moved Zach out of the way and said, "Watch the little ones my husband." She then asked Little Dove to warm a large pot of water. Sun Flower's eyes were wide, Zach thought he saw a look of fear in them. Even though he had never seen her fear anything since they had first met. She hadn't spoken a word since she dropped the bowl, but everyone in the lodge knew she'd had a severe labor pain.

Several minutes passed as Raven Wing and Shining Star tried to make her comfortable. Shining Star had cleaned up the spilled stew and laid a cool damp piece of soft tanned antelope hide over the burn. The two of them had just relaxed when Sun Flower tensed up again. Zach watched helplessly as the contraction raked her body. Raven Wing had to remind her to breathe, not to hold her breath. Finally, Raven Wing looked at Zach and said, "Grizzly Killer, will you go get Mother?"

Zach didn't even take time to put on a coat as he set the two toddlers on the buffalo robes and stepped out into the darkness and blustering cold of a late November storm. He sprinted to the lodge of his in-laws and just as soon as White Feather heard his voice she knew it was her youngest daughter's time. Zach wrapped a robe around her and leading her by the hand they went back to the large teepee with the big grizzly painted on its side.

When they entered once again Sun Flower had relaxed, the gripping pain had eased again. Zach could still see the fear in her eyes and he knew for her to show fear, the pain had to be unbearable. There were beads of sweat across her brow as she felt the warm dampness between her legs as her water broke. Even though Sun Flower knew what was happening to her, knowing and actually feeling it was completely different.

White Feather had them pull the damp dress off of her and she laid there in the dim light naked waiting for the next contraction and the blinding pain that it would bring. Zach looked again at the size of her extended belly and wondered how a baby that big could pass through the small opening that had given him so much pleasure.

Her beautiful brown eye's opened wide and then closed tight again as she tensed for another painful contraction. Zach could see the muscles ripple across her abdomen and when she had relaxed once again, White Feather felt her belly for the position of the baby. She could feel the baby's head was not all the way down into position yet and she turned to Zach and said, "Son, take the little ones to our lodge, and you and Bear Heart put them down for the night. This baby still has a long way to move before it can be born, it may take much time. You can do nothing but worry and be in our way; you should stay with Bear Heart as well."

For the first time since the contractions began Sun Flower spoke, saying, "No, Mother, I want Grizzly Killer here with me, I want him to see his child born." White Feather had a bewildered look on her face, not understanding why, but she didn't argue with her youngest child.

She just nodded then turned to Zach and said, "Grizzly Killer, take the children to their grandfather and then return." Zach smiled at his mother-in-law and nodded, even though this was his home, he wasn't about to argue with White Feather; he was going to do as she instructed.

Jimbo had been curled up just to the side of the entrance ever since he and Zach had returned from the knoll. Zach, with Little Dove's help, got the two toddlers bundled up in their warm rabbit fur blankets. Jimbo went out with him. He knew it was his job to watch over the children if Zach wasn't around and he would not let them out of his sight. Zach then noticed he hadn't seen Luna all evening and wondered where the beautiful white wolf had gone.

Bear Heart was glad to see his son-in-law again and as Zach was making up a bed for the little ones, he was also explaining to Bear Heart how much pain it looked like Sun Flower was going through. Bear Heart then told of White Feather giving birth to Sun Flower, telling Zach her last child was supposed to be the easiest but Sun Flower had been the hardest and how he had always been surprised that she was their largest baby at birth but the smallest of the three children once grown.

Zach thanked Bear Heart and looked at Jimbo who was already curled up at the children's feet and said, "Well boy, I guess there ain't no doubt about where you're spendin' the night." Bear Heart had a big smile on his face as Zach stepped back out into the cold. He, like everyone else, was amazed at the bond between Grizzly Killer and the Great Medicine Dog. Now he could see that bond extended from the big dog to his whole family.

Zach picked up an armload of wood for the inside fire before he stepped back inside his teepee. Not much had changed since he had left. He smiled at Sun Flower. Shining Star sat down by his side, leaned her head onto his shoulder and said, "There hasn't been any more of the pains since you left. I fear White Feather is right; this may take a long time."

Sun Flower wanted her husband by her side, so Zach moved over next to her. He held her hand, and it appeared she had started to doze off. The other women were all setting around the fire and Zach too, being warm and tired, started to relax when suddenly Sun Flower's grip on his hand made him sit right up. He could see the muscles in her jaw was tense as she gritted her teeth against the pain. It took only a moment for Raven Wing and White Feather to be with her while Shining Star and Little Dove awaited instructions for anything Raven Wing might need.

Once the pain subsided Sun Flower, with her eyes still closed said, in a weak voice, "That was the worst one so far."

It was White Feather that answered, saying, "My child, I fear they will get even worse before this baby of yours comes."

It was now well past midnight. Sun Flower had been in labor for over six hours and still White Feather couldn't tell if the baby's head had moved down at all. So far the pains had been irregular, coming at no set time between each one. About an hour before sunrise, that changed.

Sun Flower was tired and weak. She started to wonder how much longer she could take these blinding pains. They were coming now every few minutes, and it felt to her that with each new pain they became worse. By the time Zach could see light in the cloudy sky through the smoke hole, the pains were becoming more frequent. White Feather was now more than a little concerned for her daughter, for she could still feel the baby's head and it just wasn't moving.

Sun Flower then gripped Zach's hand again so hard it actually hurt his big strong fingers and she let out a soft moan and Raven Wing said, "I can see it, I can see the baby's head." One more terrible pain and with Sun Flower pushing with all her strength the baby came squishing out into Raven Wing's waiting hands. Shining Star had a piece of rawhide cut and waiting to tie off the umbilical cord and handed it to Raven Wing as soon as White Feather had taken the tiny baby girl.

Another contraction and the afterbirth came next. Sun Flower heard the baby cry and looked up at Zach and then at her mother as White Feather laid the tiny girl onto Sun Flower's swollen breasts. Zach smiled at seeing his baby daughter then gently wiped the beads of sweat from his wife's pretty face. He could now see relief and pride in her eyes, but most of all, he could see exhaustion.

Raven Wing cleaned up after the afterbirth but noticed something was not right. Sun Flower's belly was still huge, and she saw the muscles ripple with another contraction just as Sun Flower felt the next pain rake her body. White Feather picked up the infant and Shining Star was right there to take her as Sun Flower asked in a panicked voice what is happening and the urge to push was so great she couldn't resist.

Raven Wing answered, "You are going to have a baby little sister." No one said a word as another contraction made her push even harder, and for the second time in an hour Raven Wing announced, "It's coming, I can see its head."

This time it was Little Dove working as fast as she could cutting another piece of rawhide since Shining Star was gently rocking back and forth on her knee's holding Grizzly Killer's newest child. Zach was still by Sun Flower's side with her squeezing his hand as the contraction intensified. With one final tremendous push a second child was born. They were all in shock, none more than Zach. He looked at the tiny baby boy in Raven Wing's hands and watched White Feather take this second baby from her. Raven Wing then tied off the cord with the rawhide Little Dove handed her as Sun Flower laid back totally exhausted from her all night ordeal.

Zach thought back to the dream where his new baby was first a girl and then a boy. He had never considered the possibility of having both.

Chapter 14

Into the Unknown

SPOTTED ELK HELD UP his hand to halt the men. He then slowly moved forward toward the remains. The eyes of every hunter were scanning the entire basin for any sign of movement. It was Red Hawk that first pointed to movement across the lake and there was a quick moment of nearly silent laughter as it was just a porcupine climbing down a large spruce.

The mangled body was over half eaten away. Teeth marks had penetrated the skull and broke a large piece of it off, they were sure that is what had killed the young warrior. The bear had eaten all of his vital organs and the face was so mutilated not one of them could identify what remained.

High Back Bull stepped forward and knelt down to the bloody mangled corpse. There was a small rawhide thong still around his neck. It was so blood soaked no one else had even noticed it was there. High Back Bull took his knife and cut off the thong, pulling it free. Buried in the blood and dirt under the body was a small wooden carving of a dog howling to the heavens. Long Lance had carved the small totem and given it to his son when he was just twelve summers old and Howling Dog never removed it, it was his most prized possession.

High Back Bull just stared for a moment out across the lake; the only sound was the whispering of the breeze through the trees. The lakes surface was surprisingly calm with the approaching storm. He was trying to blink the tears away before he faced the others as he stared into the distance. A fish hit the surface of the water, which was strange for this time of the year. The fish were usually in the depths of the lakes by now where the water was slightly warmer rather than up near the surface. High Back Bull watched the ripples disappear then turned around and showed the rest of them what he held in his hand.

Everyone knew what the totem was, even Grub, Ely, and Benny, for Howling Dog had boasted about it many times. Although they all had little doubt before, this small hand carved totem positively identified Howling Dog. Red Hawk stepped forward and put his hand on High Back Bull's shoulder showing his sympathy to a man he had known his whole life.

Spotted Elk turned and looked around at the fourteen solemn faces all watching. He then spoke to them all, but looking right at the sorrowful young man, he said, "High Back Bull, I want you to pick five men to take Howling Dog's Body back to the glade and bury him with his leg. There are enough warriors here to both track the bear and honor your friend with a Shoshone Burial. Make a fire, burn the sweet sage and let the sacred smoke carry your prayers to the one above. When you have finished, return to the village and let Long Lance and Charging Bull know what you have done. But take care, all of you. The killer bear is still in the forest. Do not forget he is out there."

High Back Bull didn't speak for a minute; he was afraid his voice would break. He looked at Red Hawk and was almost surprised when Red Hawk nodded that he would go. Next he looked at Benny and said, "Benny, like Red Hawk, you have much skill with your rifle. Will you come to help keep us safe?"

Benny stood proud as he spoke, "You honor me with your words, High Back Bull. It will be my honor to go with you."

High Back Bull looked among the faces that were all looking at him and asked, "Will Standing Deer, Red Elk, and Three Feathers join us?" They all nodded, although High Back Bull knew none of these young men that were going with him were close to his loud and boastful friend, he knew they would all honor him for his journey to the land beyond.

While the five of them were carefully wrapping what was left of Howling Dog in a robe, a strange feeling came over Running Wolf. He could see Luna in his mind standing on the edge of a cliff. He shook his head and rubbed his eyes but the image would not pass. He knew his spirit helper was trying to tell him something, but he did not know what.

Ely had walked along the edge of the lake shore in both directions and although it was evident the big grizzly had been here many times, he could not tell for sure which way to go. They decided to split up and circle the lake. Ely and Grub took most of the men with them, heading around the lake to the south where it was more open, while Running Wolf, Spotted Elk, and Otter started the climb to the north. The cliffs started only a hundred yards north of them and they had to take a route out into the thick forest and away from the cliffs to get around them.

Running Wolf couldn't shake the vision of Luna from his mind. He knew his white wolf was trying to tell him something. Was it a warning? Was she trying to guide him? He just didn't know. As they climbed through the forest, he was getting frustrated with himself. He felt he wasn't able to open his heart to understand his spirit helper.

They were a hundred yards back in the forest from the edge of the cliff over the lake when they reached the top. It was then when Spotted Elk looked at Running Wolf and said, "What is it, my brother? What is troubling you?"

Running Wolf looked at Spotted Elk and then at Otter and told them what he had seen in his mind at the lakes edge. It was Otter that spoke first, "Stay here and clear your mind while Spotted Elk and myself walk to the edge. Open your heart to the message of your spirit helper, Running Wolf, for the spirit of the white wolf will not lead you wrong."

Running Wolf watched the two of them walk down the steep slope toward the edge of the cliff then he sat down crossing his legs. He had his bow and quiver rolled in his sleeping robe slung over his back and Zach's .54 caliber Hawken across his lap. He looked around him one more time and then closed his eyes and cleared all of his thoughts so he may be able to understand the message from Luna.

It was only a moment before he heard a wolf howl off in the distance and he couldn't tell if the howl was real or just in his thoughts. His mind saw her as a tiny puppy that Jimbo had watched over when Grizzly Killer had first brought her home. He then saw the giant grizzly stand up out of the oak brush on Weber's River and remembered how many shots it had taken to stop that man killing bear. He remembered Luna running to his aid and then for help when he had been dragged by the frightened pack horse just last spring.

The vision came back. He could see her standing in front of a den; the entrance protected by a large fallen tree. Her head was high, and it was as if she was looking right at him. He blinked and the vision changed. She was standing on the edge of a cliff. As he watched, he could see himself with Spotted Elk and Otter on the cliff, but Luna was gone. Suddenly an overwhelming feeling of danger came over him and he opened his eyes and looked all around. He stood up and turned around, the feeling of danger even stronger now. He started toward the cliff where he knew Spotted Elk and Otter would be. He had gone only a few yards when he heard a huffing growl and turned to see the huge bear coming through the trees toward him.

His mind was now rushing. He knew one shot would never stop the huge bear, and he didn't have time to aim, shoot, and run. So he took off on a dead run yelling, at the others the bear was right behind him. The bear was only ten yards behind Running Wolf when Spotted Elk and Otter saw him coming through the trees. Spotted Elk shouldered his rifle and fired but the grizzly didn't even flinch. Running Wolf didn't slow down as he jumped off the cliff into the unknown, followed immediately by Spotted Elk and Otter.

Grub, Ely, and the others were straight across the lake when they heard Spotted Elk's shot. Every one of them looked up just in time to see the three men splash into the ice cold water under the cliffs.

The water, only a slight degree from being ice, took his breath away as Running Wolf's feet hit the soft sandy bottom only ten feet below the surface. He bent his legs absorbing the shock and pushed off trying to reach the surface only a few feet above his head. Their heavy winter clothing, rifles, and gear made it nearly impossible for them to reach the life giving air above the water, but with extraordinary effort from a powerful will to live all three of their heads broke the surface of the near frozen lake.

All of the others ran back toward the three men as they struggled to reach the shore. Buffalo Heart was the first to reach them, stripping off his coat and pack as he ran. He didn't hesitate running into the freezing water to help. Standing Deer was just a few yards behind and he too rushed out into the lake, breaking the thin film of ice along the edge.

Spotted Elk was the first to reach the shallower water which was up just past Buffalo Heart's waist. Once he had his feet on the bottom Buffalo Heart moved to help Running Wolf while Standing Deer had to go into the deeper water to help Otter.

By the time the five of them were all out of the lake, their teeth were chattering from the cold and the others were building a large fire not far from the lake's shore. Snow from the approaching storm was falling again, this time heavier than before. While the five wet men stripped out of their buckskins, Grub and Ely started two more fires. Partially for the warmth they would provide and partially to keep the killer bear at bay.

The light faded fast as the snow got heavier. Their campsite, not far from the lake was protected by several towering pines, but some of the gusting winds was still getting through to the bare skin of the five nearly frozen men. Those with dry sleeping robes wrapped the naked men in them. Standing on the downwind side of the fire, they slowly started to warm back up.

Ely wanted to go up to where the bear had chased them off the cliff to see if he could tell a direction the grizzly was heading and see if there was blood where Spotted Elk may have wounded him before the falling snow covered all sign, but Grub, Otter, and Spotted Elk all talked him out of it. In the fading light they believed it was just too dangerous.

After building drying racks to drape the wet buckskins and robes over, they all sat between the three large fires and ate cold wet jerky from Spotted Elk, Otter, and Running Wolf's pouches, and talked about what had happened and what they would do come morning.

*****

Benny and Red Hawk led the solemn procession back down through the rocky gorge into the thick timber of the ravine. It was nearly dark by the time they reached the glade. There was an inch of new fallen snow on top of the frozen horses as they entered the clearing and, without saying anything, they all knew this is where they would spend the night.

All six of these men were young, at nineteen summers Benny and Red Hawk were the oldest, but they all, except Benny, had been raised with the dangers of the wilderness all around them and for the last couple of years, Benny had been taught how to survive this rugged country by the very best: Grub, Ely, and Zach.

Red Hawk suggested, "Let us move to the far side of the glade away from the dead horses, in case the bear comes back to feed." After setting the heavy pack down that contained the remains of Howling Dog, they all headed to the far side. Red Elk and Standing Deer started on a fire while Three Feathers and Red Hawk started gathering the wood they would need to feed the fire through the night.

Benny just stood there looking all around, then he too started to work building another fire several feet away. By the time they had a substantial amount of wood gathered, Red Elk and Standing Deer had a fire crackling through the small pine branches above their dry tinder.

Once their fire was burning well, Red Elk took a burning branch and started Benny's fire with it. They set up a third fire as well but decided not to light it until they laid down for the night. With plenty of time, Three Feathers suggested they cut some meat off of one of the horses instead of just having dry hard jerky for their meal, so he and Red Hawk walked back across the glade. It took quite an effort to skin and cut the nearly frozen meat from the back strap of one of the frozen horses.

Just as they were finishing an uneasy feeling came over them; first Red Hawk and then Standing Deer. Both men looked up, their eyes trying to penetrate the thick forest in the rapidly fading light. Red Hawk whispered, "Something is out there." Standing Deer simply nodded as they both stood up and walked backwards toward their burning fires.

Standing Deer handed the meat to High Back Bull who had sticks ready for the fresh meat but he and Red Hawk continued watching all around them. Benny stood up next to his friends and asked, "What is it Red Hawk?"

Red Hawk shook his head as he said, "Don't know, but it felt like we were being watched."

At hearing that, Benny took a burning log from his fire and started their third fire then asked, "Do you figure this is enough or should we light another one?" They looked around at the others who, without saying a word, started building another fire. All of them had seen what the bear had done to Howling Dog and none of them wanted to take any chances that the killer bear would come near them through the night.

They ate the stringy horse meat, not sure it was any better than the dried buffalo they carried would have been, but at least it was hot. After they ate they went into the dark forest as a group. While Benny and Red Hawk stood guard with their

117

rifles, the others dragged in enough wood to keep all four fires burning through the night.

They were jumpy, and none felt like lying down, so the six of them sat between the fires and watched out into the blackness as a very light snow continued to fall. By the time the first light of day had started to lighten the dark gray clouds above them, the snow had stopped. No more than another inch had fallen in the glade during the night. None of these six young men had slept during the night and each one was glad daylight was nearly upon them.

While they waited for full daylight, they heated up the remaining horse meat and filled their empty bellies. Suddenly, Red Hawk dropped his meat and cocked the rifle that Grizzly Killer had given him years ago. They all turned to where Red Hawk was looking and as Benny turned he too cocked his rifle and brought it to his shoulder. In the dim light of early dawn, on the far side of the glade standing on his hind legs was the largest bear any of them had ever seen.

Benny and Red Hawk had heard the stories of the huge killer bear that Grizzly Killer, Running Wolf, and three Shoshone hunters had killed on Weber's River. Although neither of them realized just how big a grizzly could be. This was the first grizzly Benny had ever seen and though the others had seen grizzlies before, none of them had ever seen anything this big.

The bear was on the far side of the horses, much too far to shoot at, and he appeared to be as large as the horses were. Standing there erect the top of his head was ten feet above the ground and he was staring directly at the four burning fires with the six men between them.

A gust of wind blew a thin cloud of snow from the dead horses and just for an instant obscured their view of the giant bear and as the snow settled the bear was gone. Benny strained to see but there was nothing there. Not one of them had seen the bear stand up and not one had seen him leave. Red Hawk looked at Benny and asked, "Was he really there?" Benny just nodded and they started looking into the forest all around them.

Standing Deer started adding more wood to their fires and none of them wanted to step out from between the protective flames.

Chapter 15

The Hunters Return

AS MORNING DAWNED, the sky was still dark and dreary, so far the storm had left only a skiff of snow. In the lodge of Grizzly Killer there was joy; the tiny twins and their mother were doing just fine. Sun Flower had suckled the babies and now both mother and babies were asleep. Zach was sitting next to Shining Star as he watched over them all. Star, Gray Wolf, and Jimbo were still in the lodge with their grandfather and White Feather and Raven Wing had just left to go there. Shining Star looked up into Zach's tired blue eyes and smiled. She could see the joy and pride he felt. He smiled back at her, put his arm around her and pulled her even closer. Then together the two of them laid back. Little Dove had laid down as well and within minutes everyone in the lodge was asleep.

Jimbo stood as White Feather and Raven Wing entered the lodge of Bear Heart. He knew the children were safe, and he had others to protect as well. He waited until Raven Wing had checked on the two toddlers, then push his way through the flap and headed back to Zach's teepee.

He pushed through the flap and walked past his sleeping master and took in the smell of the latest members of his family. He now had two more little ones to protect and everyone knew he would protect them with his life. He looked at Zach lying there with Shining Star's head on his shoulder. The big dog was torn between loyalties at that moment. He, like the rest, knew Luna was about to have his puppies and he also knew she had left to find a den for her new family. The call of the wild was strong in the white wolf, and like her mother before her, she would go off to give birth by herself.

Knowing his human family was safe, Jimbo pushed through the door flap of Zach's lodge and into the dim light of the gray morning. It had been hours since Luna had left the village but Jimbo had no trouble following her faint scent. She had gone nearly four miles downstream and found where a badger had dug out a large area under a downed cottonwood as it dug for one of the many moles in this area. Luna finished digging it out, making the den large enough for her to have her puppies.

Jimbo couldn't see her as he stood outside of the den but he knew she was there and the whining of six tiny puppies let him know he now had another family to protect. He laid there, guarding the entrance for a time then left for his morning hunt. He wasn't gone long when he brought a cottontail rabbit back and dropped it in the entrance to the den. He then left going back to check on his humans.

With his long legs, and ability to run all day, the four miles back to the village took less than fifteen minutes. He pushed his way through the entrance flap and saw Sun Flower was sitting up suckling the twins again. He slowly approached her, smelling the new scents once again. Sun Flower smiled and softly spoke to him, "Jimbo, these are our babies." She lifted the tiny boy from her nipple and held him out for the big dog to see. Jimbo reached out and gently licked the side of his head and Sun Flower knew as long as the Great Medicine Dog was here her babies would be safe.

*****

It had taken hours for Running Wolf and the others to stop shaking from the cold. The gusting wind and steady snow hadn't helped. They had kept the fires burning hot but with the falling snow melting before morning all of their robes were soaked through.

The lake was high enough in the mountains that the snow was much heavier up here and by daylight there was nearly eight inches of the white fluffy snow on the ground. They all knew there would be nothing left of the tracks from the day before to follow so unless they found fresh tracks in the snow this morning, this hunt was over.

Running Wolf's buckskins were mostly dry but even where they weren't they were warm as he put them back on. While he and the others dressed, Ely, Grub, and the others spread out to see if they could find any tracks in the fresh snow.

They found tracks of nearly every animal that lived in the forest except bear. Grub came across the tracks of a large cougar that appeared to be following a deer. From mice to snowshoe hares, the fresh snow showed the forest was overflowing with life. Ely walked up on the broad wing marks of a great horned owl that had dived into the snow for a mouse just before light. Up above the cliffs he found where a lobo wolf had stood on the edge, looking out over the basin, but there was no sign of the bear.

They searched for over two hours then met the others back at the fires. With nothing to follow, they had no choice but to head back to their village. Once there, they would decide whether to go out again or wait until the bear shows himself. They all hoped this new snow would force the killer bear into his den for the winter.

They started back down, at first crossing the basin and then they started down the narrow rocky gorge. With the trail hidden under the snow, the large boulders were treacherous. Being extremely slippery, they were very hard to climb down. It took them over twice as long to maneuver their way back down the gorge as it had taken them to climb up through it just the day before. Grub pointed out the trail of smoke coming from the glade far below while they were still above the dense forest below the gorge.

The snow wasn't nearly as deep once they reached the thick trees, and it was a relief to all once they cleared the treacherously slick gorge. The forest was eerily quiet once again but none of them knew if it was because of the storm or if the great predator was near. The canopy of towering pines had stopped most of the snow from reaching the soft thick layer of pine needles that made up the forest floor. It made walking much easier, but the tall spruce and pines also cut out much of the light that was already limited by the thick layer of gray clouds above.

As they got closer to the glade, they could smell the smoke from the fires, and as they walked into the opening, they were only fifty yards from the dead frozen horses. They stopped and looked across the glade at the four fires with their friends still within the circle of flames. After actually seeing the size of the giant bear, none of them wanted to chance coming face to face with him with only Benny and Red Hawk's rifles. None of them believed their arrows would ever stop the grizzly. Now they had many more rifles; Grub, Ely, Spotted Elk, and Otter all carried them.

Benny smiled a big broad smile; Grub and Ely were back with him. These two old mountain men were not only his partners, they were the men that had taught him nearly everything he knew about living in the Rockies and he always felt better when he was with them.

They met in the middle of the glade and it took only moments after hearing the story that they were all on alert and slowly walking to the far side of where two of the scattered horses were lying only a few feet apart. Red Elk had told them that the bear was standing at the edge of the trees behind those two frozen horses.

The men were bunched together and watching the trees all around the glade as they moved toward the spot. They all knew if they could find the tracks, the hunt would be on again. Ely moved ahead of the rest and held up his hand for them all to stop. He didn't want any sign or track stepped on even by mistake, but there was nothing there. The wind had been gusting all morning and swirling the light powdery snow. When he could find no sign at all, he called Grub over and the two of them started walking circles but there was no sign the big bear had been there. Red Hawk looked at Benny with a questioning look and those two looked at High Back Bull and the others. They all nodded, every one of them had seen the bear, but there was no trace of him at all.

After they had looked for over an hour, they still found no trace. They all gathered and laid the remains of Howling Dog with the already covered leg. They built a small fire and lit a small, tightly wound bundle of sage. High Back Bull held the smoking sage and prayed silently as he moved the bundle with its sacred smoke in the four directions and then to the sky above and earth below, waving the tendrils of smoke over his head so it would carry his prayer to the one above. Even though Howling Dog had been disgraced, for the sake of the living, they all took part in praying for a fallen Shoshone Warrior. Just as the last one of them finished, a lone wolf high on the mountain howled a long and mournful farewell that carried down through the trees to them all. A chill ran down Benny's back, and he was sure that was God's way of telling them their prayers had been heard.

By the time they were finished, they guessed they had less than an hour of daylight left. They still had to find their horses, wherever they had wandered to, and make the twenty-mile ride back to the village. They decided to stay there in the glade one more night since the four fires were still burning and the snow all around them had melted. They didn't have to make a camp and none of them knew how long it was going to take to find the horses.

They brought in more than enough fire wood to keep all four fires burning through the night and sliced off more of the horse meat and got it cooking. Grub, looking into the fire that he, Ely, Benny, and Running Wolf were sitting by said, "Ya know, I'd give half my plews from the fall hunt for a pot of hot coffee right now."

Ely chuckled as he nodded and said, "Sure would be the most costly pot ya ever did make, but it just might be worth it at that."

Benny laughed at the two of them and told them both, "You two is crazy, ain't nothin' worth that much."

Grub looked up from the flames at his young partner and said, "You just wait another twenty year or so youngster, an' you might be singing a different tune."

Ely nodded, and said, "That's fer sure, pard."

The night passed quietly with two of them at a time standing guard and keeping the fires burning. None of them had slept any the night before so even though the temperature dropped significantly through the night as the clouds slowly cleared, the guards kept the fires burning and the tired men slept. They changed guards every couple of hours so all of them got the much need rest they needed.

As morning dawned, the air was bitter cold; the fires kept the worst of it away if they could stay close enough. Ely looked at his lifelong partner and said, "This mornin' I'd throw all my plews in if'n the pot was big enough."

Benny just shook his head and smiled at the two of them and thought, *"I might just throw some in myself for a good hot cup 'bout now."* Although after what he said about that the night before, he didn't tell either one of them that.

As they started out, Grub reminded them all that the bear was still out there so keep a sharp eye out as they headed back through the forest. It didn't take them long to hike through the dense spruce and pines. They were so much lower on the mountains now that there was little snow and almost none had reached the forest floor. As they left the thick trees, the sun had come out from behind the clouds that still covered much of the eastern third of the sky. Each man squinted from its brightness as they moved out on to the open valley floor.

They were tired and cold as they marched toward the edge of the brush where they expected to find their horses. They all knew the horses would have moved; they would try to find good grass and a place out of the cold wind. None of them expected the horses to go as far as they did.

They finally found them nearly three miles from where they left them. In the same wash and not all that far from where the first bunch of horses had ran to after the bear attacked. They were scattered out for a quarter mile down through the wash but it didn't take long to round them up. Standing Deer's pinto was the closest and once he was mounted, he was able to round up the others in no time.

A bit over two hours later they rode into the village and the first thing that they saw was most everyone gathered around the large teepee of Grizzly Killer. Running Wolf kicked his chestnut into a lope, worried about what had happened.

When he got closer, he could see Zach and all four women, along with Bear Heart and White Feather, was at the center and everyone there was smiling. They cleared a path for Running Wolf but right behind him were the rest of them coming to see what was happening.

Raven Wing rushed to Running Wolf and Butterfly to Spotted Elk. Red Hawk saw Meadowlark and as he looked at her, she looked away. He was hurt and didn't understand why she was afraid to let anyone know the feelings they had for one another.

Running Wolf saw the baby Sun Flower was holding and joy filled his heart. He like everyone that was close to her knew how long she had wanted this. Then he noticed White Feather was holding another tiny infant, and he hadn't been aware anyone else in the village was expecting. He greeted Zach with a hug and then Sun Flower, she could see the question in his eyes and she smiled as she nodded, saying, "Yes, my husband's medicine is so great the one above has blessed us with two babies, the first a girl and the next a boy.

Everyone in the village was in a festive mood. All but Long Lance; his heart was sad over the loss of his son. Even though he knew Howling Dog had brought it all on himself it was hard for him to say goodbye.

Before the celebration and feast they planned for later in the day, Charging Bull called a council where the story of the bear and finding Howling Dog was relayed to everyone in the village. Long Lance was grateful to them all that they had given him a warriors farewell, and even a tear ran down his wrinkled old face as High Back Bull gave him the totem that he himself had carved so many years ago.

Everyone was concerned as they told of jumping off the cliff into the ice-cold water of the lake, hearing of landing in the water made nearly everyone there shiver some just thinking about it.

Knowing the bear was still out there and roaming free made everyone in the village feel as if they were all in danger. Charging Bull decided right then they would all guard the village much closer until they knew the bear was gone.

Zach was so proud of his twin babies and their mother, he wouldn't have left for anything, but how he wished he could have been there with his partner and friends. He knew the outcome probably wouldn't have been any different, but he still had the feeling that he and Running Wolf together could take on anything the wilderness could throw at them. Zach knew with Jimbo along the bear could not have just vanished, the bear couldn't shed his scent and anywhere the grizzly went Zach knew Jimbo could have followed.

Chapter 16

Valley of Smoking Waters

FOR THE NEXT two weeks life in the village became much more normal. A couple more early winter storms had blown through and there was now six inches of snow in the village, but nearly that many feet in the high mountain passes. The new moon had begun. Dommo-mea', the winter moon, but to Zach it was December, almost Christmas. The killer grizzly had not shown himself again and everyone figured he had finally gone into his den for the long winters sleep.

Zach rejoiced in his growing family but now, just before Christmas, the memories of his own childhood and his Ma and Pa invaded his thoughts. How he wished they could have lived to meet his family and to play with their grandchildren. He could picture the joy his little ones would have brought his Ma, and he hoped his beliefs were correct, that his Ma and Pa could still see him and did know his family and were watching over them from above.

Luna's puppies' eyes were now open, but she still kept them warm and safe deep inside the den. Jimbo brought her food each morning, a rabbit, grouse or ground hog, whatever he could catch on his morning hunts. No one but Luna had seen the puppies yet, not even Jimbo had been allowed inside the den. Jimbo had made so many trips between the village and the den he had a hard-packed trail through the snow. Zach and Running Wolf had visited the den several times and Luna would come to the opening of the den to greet them but would not come out so they could see the puppies.

Two more weeks passed and winter had fully gripped the valley of the Wind River. Another new moon, goa-mea', the freezing moon, had risen and the bitter cold had everything in the land frozen. Zach and Sun Flower's twin babies were growing fast but Sun Flower was finding she wasn't producing enough milk to feed both of the hungry infants and was thankful that Shining Star, who was still supplementing what Star was eating with her milk, was able to supply the additional milk that Sun Flower lacked.

A month had passed since the bear had chased Running Wolf, Spotted Elk, and Otter off the cliff. Life in the village was now lived mostly inside the warm lodges. They had used up all the firewood in the area around the village and were having to drag in logs from great distances or they would freeze. Everyone knew it was time to move the village even though no one wanted to in the bitter January cold.

Benny, Red Hawk, and Buffalo Heart were out hunting every day that it wasn't storming. Sometimes just the three of them but more often than not Standing Deer, Red Elk, High Back Bull, and Three Feathers joined them. Sometimes they would stay out a night or even two as they tried the take enough fresh meat to feed the village.

Those seven young men were not the only ones hunting; Grub and Ely braved the cold winter air frequently but they were always back to the warmth of their lodge and Little Doves cooking by the time the sun dropped behind the towering peaks of the Wind River Mountains. Zach and Running Wolf, Spotted Elk, Otter, and others as well hunted most days that the cold maker was resting and not bringing in more vicious storms. It took extreme effort from everyone to keep the entire village fed through dommo-mea', the freezing moon. Most days the hunters returned empty handed; the game had been driven away by the snow. They continued hunting but it became harder and harder to find the needed meat. This was yet another sign the village must be moved.

A council was held, smoke from the sacred pipe carried their prayers to the one above as they sought guidance in where they would find both ample wood for their fires and game would be plentiful for their hunters. It seemed each one had a different opinion as to where to move but most of the elders believed they needed to go south away from the Wind River to the Sweetwater or beyond.

Raven Wing had a dream in the early morning hours of that day but it had taken much of the day before she understood what the dream meant. She seen a great celebration in the village. Everyone was eating and there was more meat roasting on the fires. She then was bathing in water so warm it took time for her cold skin to get used to it. Finally, she could see Running Wolf, and then her sister and Zach, each with a baby in their arms, and then she saw Shining Star with Star as the slight breeze moved around the heavy layer of steam that looked like smoke on the water. Then there was Luna, the white wolf was standing on the rock above the smoking water and she realized it was her husband's spirit helper that had showed her this vision.

The council was nearly over when Raven Wing realized where the village must move. They must follow the river to the place of the Smoking Waters on the far side of the steep rocky gorge where the Wind River cut through the mountain as it found its way north toward the mighty Elk River, or as the white men called it the Yellowstone. She carried Gray Wolf as she walked to the council fire where everyone in the village was waiting for their decision. Although every person there was allowed to speak at the council, most did not, trusting Charging Bull and the elders to make the right decision for the well-being of the village.

As Raven Wing approached, the men made a pathway for her to where the elders where seated around the fire. Everyone had stopped talking when she approached, knowing this must be something very important for her to interrupt the council.

Charging Bull looked up at her and then at her father, Bear Heart, who was seated in his usual spot next to his son Spotted Elk. It was plain for him to see Bear Heart was just as puzzled as he was.

Charging Bull asked, "What is it, Raven Wing? What has brought you to this council?"

Raven Wing, after apologizing for interrupting said, "My Chief, I had a dream early this morning. I saw our village; there was meat roasting on all the fires and everyone was happy. I saw myself and all of my family bathing in the pools of smoking water north of the canyon of the Wind River. I believe it was the white wolf that showed me this in my dream, and I believe if we follow the wolf's direction we will find everything we need until the Sun once again drives the cold maker from our land."

The council was silent as they pondered over what Raven Wing had just said. They all knew it was a hard and treacherous journey for over fifty miles to reach the springs of Smoking Waters of which Raven Wing spoke. Finally it was Blue Fox, the old Medicine Man, that spoke, his voice soft and weak. His sight so poor he could no longer see the woman standing before them, but everyone there heard his every word, "I am old, maybe too old for such a difficult move, but I believe Raven Wing is right. You all know of her power and her strength. I taught her as a child about the healing plants and how to use them, but the one above has given her the vision, the power to see what others cannot. Yes, we should follow the white wolf. We should follow the vision of the most powerful Shaman I have ever met, Raven Wing."

Many, including Raven Wing was stunned by his last remark. Although everyone knew of her healing powers and many believed her to be a Shaman as well, for Blue Fox to say she was the most powerful he had met in his long life elevated her to a whole new level of respect and there wasn't a man at the council that would not follow her vision.

Bear Heart was filled with pride; his oldest, Spotted Elk, sat next to their chief as War Chief, protector of their people, and his oldest daughter became a powerful Shaman, even though she herself had never considered her that. After hearing the words of Blue Fox, the man the Shoshone people had known for all of their lives as a powerful healer and Shaman, everyone in the village would see Raven Wing as their new Shaman from now on.

Raven Wing stood there silent just behind the ring of elders sitting around the council fire. Everyone including Running Wolf and Zach was waiting for her to speak, but the words would not come. She was worried now. What if she led her people wrong? Although Blue Fox's sight was not much more than a blur, in his mind he could now see Raven Wing holding her child clearly and it was he that spoke again, his voice stronger now than just a moment before. "Raven Wing, do not doubt what the one above has shown you, or what he will show you in the future. Use your knowledge, listen to your heart, follow your visions, and never doubt what you see and feel is real."

Running Wolf walked up to her and took the squirming child from her arms. Although she was still speechless, she felt an inner strength start burning within her. Raven Wing had never wanted power, she had only ever wanted to help her family and her people. Even though she knew she would be leaving with her family to go back to their home on Black's Fork once the grass started to turn green again, she would do everything within her power to help this village thrive.

Although they weren't in danger of running out of food right now, everyone in the village knew that without fresh meat and a lot of it their supply of dried buffalo from the fall hunts wouldn't last more than another month or so. Charging Bull sent word to every lodge that they would be moving to the place of the Smoking Waters when the sun has risen three more times.

Zach had been amazed how fast Sun Flower had recovered from giving birth and although it had been only six weeks she had lost much of her extra weight. The family was happy; Star loved her little brother and sister and other than Sun Flower not having enough milk for both rapidly growing babies, everything was great. Between Shining Star and Raven Wing both being able to suckle them, neither of the twins were ever hungry.

The day before they were going the leave, Zach, Running Wolf, Benny, Grub, and Ely were all going through the pack saddles, inspecting and repairing. Rodents had chewed through the rawhide straps in several places. Running Wolf got a strange feeling, and only a moment later Raven Wing stepped out of their teepee. She had a strange look on her face and asked, "Running Wolf is something wrong?" Running Wolf stood and now all the others were looking around as Jimbo came trotting toward them from his well-worn trail to the den. But this time Luna was right behind him and following her were six of the prettiest puppies any of them had ever seen.

Zach burst out laughing as he watched the six week old puppies try to keep up with their mother. They were adorable little bundles of long white and gray fur, with little black noses and wagging tales. Soon word had spread throughout the village that the great medicine dog's puppies were out and before long Running Wolf and Raven Wing's teepee was surrounded with villagers wanting to see the great dog's puppies. Luna, however wasn't pleased with all the attention. She bared her teeth at all the people even as Jimbo was greeting them. Raven Wing opened the teepee flap, and she jumped through with the six puppies struggling behind her to climb up over the lip and into the lodge.

For the rest of that day, those six puppies were the center of most conversations around the village as everyone prepared to leave the next morning. Many of the people wanted one of the great medicine dogs pups, believing Jimbo's strong medicine would be passed down to them.

Since the puppies were too small to make the fifty-mile trek on their own, Zach and Running Wolf put together packs for one of the horses that would hold three of the little furry puppies on each side. Neither of them was sure how Luna was going to like the pups not being with her but they really had no other choice.

The next morning dawned cold and clear, it was barely light as teepees started coming down all over the village. The heavy buffalo hide lodges were rolled up and placed on travoises along with everything else that was inside the lodges. Even the totems that most had set up outside the teepees were loaded onto travoises to make the trip to where they all believed they would spend the rest of the winter.

Sun Flower had spent most of the day before making a second cradle board now that she had two babies to carry. The babies were wrapped in warm rabbit fur blankets and then in a Hudson Bay style wool blanket. Zach had tied the two cradle boards together and sized them so they would fit over Sun Flower's blanket saddle and ride next to the warm sides of her horse. The wool blankets were then folded down over the top of them to keep the cold air away from their little faces.

It was the unmarried men that would push the large horse herd; Red Hawk and Buffalo Heart were among the oldest of them. Red Hawk and Meadowlark had not spent nearly as much time together over the last few weeks since winter had really set in and Red Hawk had started wondering if he had done something wrong. It seemed like she was all he ever thought about. Even while they were out hunting his mind was on Meadowlark and the way she made him feel. He had decided he would offer Wind in His Face five horses for her to marry him once the village was resettled at the hot springs.

The puppies loved to play, and Gray Wolf and Star both loved them. Luna watched her puppies and her children play together as the travoises were tied onto the horses and loaded. She wasn't nearly as patient though as Running Wolf and Zach started packing the whining pups into the packs that they would ride to their new home in. After Running Wolf knelt down and assured her they would be fine, she seemed to understand and settled down but she never let the packs out of her sight. She walked beside the horse ever anxious for Running Wolf to lift them out of the packs every time they stopped. Sun Flower had to feed her twins every couple of hours and each time they stopped Running Wolf would indeed put the puppies down as well.

Although all six of the puppies were strong and healthy, one female was definitely smaller than the rest of them. Of the six, four were males leaving just two females. Many members of the tribe had expressed interest in having one of the puppies for their own but each time someone asked, Running Wolf would point to Luna and say, "The puppies are not mine to give; they belong to Luna. You'll have to talk to her about that." Although most thought he was just kidding with them, none of them knew for sure.

The village made good progress that first day as they followed the Wind River downstream across the broad valley. Zach figured even with the many stops they had covered over fifteen miles. Another day would bring them to the rough rocky gorge of the Wind River Canyon and he knew once they started down through the canyon, their progress would slow. They were all thankful that there was no sign of a storm but the bitter cold of winter in the north-central Rocky Mountains was hard on man and animal alike.

Old Blue Fox with his failing health and eyesight seemed to be having a harder time than anyone else in the village after just the first day. Raven Wing made up another travois and insisted he ride on it for the second day, but his pride would not allow him to do that and he insisted he would either ride his horse or he would make the journey to the land beyond. Although Raven Wing tried telling him it wasn't safe with his failed sight, the old Medicine Man smiled at her and said, "I do not have to see, my child. There is nothing wrong with my horse's eyes."

It had been many summers since Medicine Keeper had left to make the journey to the other side. She had been Blue Fox's wife ever since they were young. She had only been a child when she was found wandering the prairie alone after her Cheyenne family had been killed in a terrible battle with the crow while hunting.

She was taken in and raised as a Shoshone and eventually became the wife of their revered Medicine Man, Blue Fox. That is when she was given the name Medicine Keeper as she helped Blue Fox gather and store the healing plants that was so important to the Shoshone's health and well-being. Since her death, Blue Fox had aged tremendously and Raven Wing wondered how much longer he would be with them.

She watched him riding with his eyes closed much of that day and she wondered if he was meditating and praying or had just fallen asleep. Charging Bull stopped to camp just before the river started into the steep narrow canyon. After the fires were all set Blue Fox called for Raven Wing. With his eyes still closed and in his shaky old voice he said, "Raven Wing, I spent today riding alongside Medicine Keeper and I know my time to walk upon this earth is nearly over. My place is now at my wife's side. Let no one mourn my passing, for I will die a happy man. I know Medicine Keeper is waiting for me on the other side and I know you will carry on my work here. Raven Wing, it matters not whether you stay with the Shoshone or build your future with the Utes of your husband or build your own village with Grizzly Killer and his family. You will be a healer and a Shaman all the days of your life. Go now my child, this old man must rest." She hesitated only a moment as she watched him relax and breathe his last breath.

Chapter 17

The Hot Springs

A TEEPEE WAS erected and Blue Fox was placed inside. His body would not be left unattended until he was laid in his final resting place. Raven Wing would decide where that resting place would be, for now her word carried as much weight as Blue Fox's had for so many years. She was now going through his things, finding his finest ceremonial dress before anyone was allowed to see him. White Feather and Basket Maker both come to help her prepare his body and dress him in his finest. A teepee was erected in which to place his body for the night and fires were built both inside and outside the east facing entrance.

Once Raven Wing was satisfied her old mentor was ready to proudly ride to meet Medicine Keeper, she opened the entrance flap. Chief Charging Bull was the first to enter the lodge, he stood and stared at his old friend. He could not remember a time in his life when Blue Fox was not the Medicine Man of his people and although Charging Bull did not mourn his passing, he was sad just the same that he would not see his friend again until he too was called upon to make the journey to the other side.

Every person in the village passed through the teepee that night. They all knew that come morning, Raven Wing would find the place that Blue Fox would be buried.

Raven Wing and Spotted Elk left before full light and climbed to a place just above the steep rocky slope northwest of where the now frozen river cut the gorge through the mountain. From this high vantage place Blue Fox could see the entirety of his homeland, the Wind River Valley. He could see the morning sun rising over the mountains and plains to the east, and he would be closer to the stars and Milky Way that he would follow into the next life.

It was midday by the time the whole village had climbed to the top of the ridge where Blue Fox's body had been placed under a large overhanging rock then covered completely with stones and dirt so that nothing could ever disturb it. His faithful old horse, the only one he still owned, was led up to the grave and held while Charging Bull held the lead rope. Spotted Elk in a swift and painless motion cut its throat. It took only moments for the horse to bleed out and lay down in front of the grave and everyone was satisfied that now Blue Fox would have a good mount to ride into the next life.

Zach and several of the others could see a group of mountain sheep grazing on a slope less than a mile from where Blue Fox was buried. After discussing it with Charging Bull, it was decided the village would stay another night where they were at the head of the canyon and Zach along with a half dozen hunters would try to take some fresh meat.

Everyone with a rifle followed Zach while those with a bow and arrow or lance followed High Back Bull and Standing Deer. Zach led his group along the top of the cliffs above the river until they were well northeast of the sheep. They then turned back toward the unsuspecting animals, keeping a rocky spine between them.

High Back Bull and Standing Deer led those with them well below where the sheep were grazing; where they thought they would run after the hunters above fired their long rifles. Zach stopped and stepped off Ol' Red, dropping the reins to the ground knowing the mule wouldn't move from that spot. He silently crawled to the rocks at the ridge tops and, looking through the prairie grass, saw he was right where he needed to be. He backed down a few feet and motioned for Spotted Elk, Benny, Grub, Ely, and Otter to come up on both sides of him.

Five minutes later Zach felt the heavy recoil of his .54 Hawken and only moments later the entire ridge top was filled with blue gray smoke from the burning gun powder of their rifles. Five sheep were down and a sixth that was badly wounded would not go far.

The remaining sheep broke running downhill away from the thundering rifles only to meet the deadly arrows of the other hunters. The hunt was a great success. Of the two dozen or so sheep in the herd, the hunters had taken nine of them. Tonight, everyone in the village would eat their fill of fresh meat.

When Zach and the other hunters returned, the women had put up lean-tos. Although they weren't nearly as warm as the teepees, with a fire right in front they were warm enough to keep the chill off and protect the babies from the bitter cold night time air.

As the sun set, the smell of roasting sheep filled the air along the banks of the river. Even though the day had been sad with the loss and burial of Blue Fox, Raven Wing's words about his last wish was that no one should mourn for him for he was ready to make the journey, and those words had really went to the heart of the people. Now, with fresh meat on the fires and a promise of a new and better place to spend the rest of the winter, everyone was cheerful tonight.

Zach sat by the fire and watched his two wives suckle the two tiny babies and then Star, though Star wasn't depending on the nourishing milk from her mother all the time now.

As they laid down for the night, all of them under the same heavy buffalo robes, they could hear both wolves and coyotes on the ridge where they had taken the sheep. Zach had no doubt the gut piles from the kills would be gone by morning.

It was a narrow and rough trail through the canyon of the Wind River. In some places one of the travois poles would be riding on the ice of the frozen river. It would have been much easier if they could have traveled out on the ice but in many places the current was so swift the water was not frozen solid.

Although it was less than twenty miles from where they had camped, the rough rocky trail kept them from making good time. It would take two more days to reach the smoking waters. Jimbo wasn't content to walk along at the slow pace of the horses pulling the travois and ran on ahead of the procession to scout as he always did. Zach and Running Wolf rode ahead as well, following the big dog.

Much of the canyon sides were steep talus slopes that had filled in with dirt over eons of time and now grass and brush was growing on those slopes from the river's edge up to where the rock cliffs started. The near vertical rock walls above the slopes went up so neither man nor beast could go over them. In other places the cliffs came to the water's edge. They saw large herds of big horn sheep feeding just below the cliffs. Zach was amazed at their numbers. He figured the sheep must have come here from mountains all around to spend the winter in this rugged canyon. Hawks and eagles soared in the heights above the cliffs and as Zach looked up into the azure blue sky, he was thankful there had been no storms, and it appeared there would be none at least until the village was relocated.

They stopped a couple of hours before sunset in a place where the canyon had widened but it was still so narrow the village was spread out for over a half mile. The herders had pushed the horses on ahead as they could travel much faster than the ones pulling the travoises.

Red Hawk stopped the horses at the north end of the gorge where the country flattened out some and there was enough grass to hold them. They set up their camp along the river and would wait there the next day until the slower moving villagers caught up with them. Buffalo Heart rode to the east less than a mile when he saw a herd of antelope and was able to take one of the small prairie goats for the herders' evening meal.

140

When Buffalo Heart returned with the young buck over the back of his blanket saddle, Red Hawk was separating his own horses from the herd. Of his eleven horses he was going to pick the five best to offer Wind in His Face for Meadowlark's hand in marriage. He had not said anything about his plans to Meadowlark and was troubled whether or not he should.

He had tried to understand her reluctance to let anyone know of their relationship, he had even talked to Buffalo Heart about it, but neither understood. What neither Red Hawk nor Meadowlark knew was that nearly everyone in the village did know about it. Basket Maker had finally talked to Wind in His Face about their daughter and although at first he objected, she had laughed at him and asked him who he would choose for her. After he had considered what his wife had said he had resolved himself to the fact that his daughter was now a woman and Red Hawk was as good of a man as she would find.

Buffalo Heart just sat back and smiled at Red Hawk. He knew his friend better than anyone else and he couldn't believe he was so blinded by his feelings for Meadowlark he had not been aware of the looks and whispers throughout the village about the young couple.

He could see the turmoil in Red Hawk's mind and although tempted to tease him about it, he did not want to add to the anxiety that his lifelong friend was going through. At the same time, he couldn't help himself in letting Red Hawk fret over his decision even though he was sure Wind in His Face would except the horses for his daughter.

It was High Back Bull that first saw Jimbo well out ahead of the slow moving village. Nearly a mile behind the great medicine dog, he could see Ol' Red with Grizzly Killer riding him. The big Kentucky mule with his long ears was easy to identify even from this distance, and it was only moments later when Jimbo was among the herders. By then all the young men with the horses were together, and just minutes later Zach and Running Wolf rode up to them.

From here they were only six or seven easy miles to the hot springs and the open water of the river below where the very hot water from the cascading pools runs into the river. Zach stood in his stirrups and surveyed the land all around. He could see three different herds of antelope and with the canyon being home to so many sheep he knew Raven Wing was right in bringing the village here. There wasn't enough daylight left to make it all the way to the springs, but they moved on and camped to where they would only have a couple hours to go the next morning.

Hunters went out long before they stopped for the night and once again the village had fresh meat for the night. Even though Zach and Running Wolf, along with Grub, Ely, and Benny, didn't have time to pursue them, they were excited to see a herd of several hundred buffalo up on the flats east of the river.

The hot Springs did have a bad side as a place to camp. Their proximity to the lands of the Cheyenne, Sioux, Crow, and even the Blackfeet made these springs a frequent stopping place for hunters from the enemies of the Shoshone. Although it was very unlikely for any of their enemies to venture this far from their villages in the dead of winter, they would take extra care in setting guards around the village for as long as they were here.

Grub and Ely had been here several times and soaked in the warm mineral waters. They had traveled the length of the Big Horn River to trade their furs at Fort Benton at the confluence of the Big Horn with the Yellowstone River before General Ashley had started the Rendezvous each summer. This was the first time Zach, Running Wolf, or Benny had seen the springs in this basin surrounded by red hills and bluffs. Zach wondered why the same river had two different names after the Wind River flowed out of the canyon. It became known as the Big Horn from there until it emptied into the Yellowstone. Neither Grub nor Ely could answer him.

The village was set along the banks of the river less than a quarter mile north of the large pool of very hot water. The scalding water cooled as it flowed over the limestone terraces into pools below and finally into the river itself. The hot water kept the river ice-free downstream for a ways and from the village the women had easy access to water, and the hunters had easy access to the vast hunting grounds of the Big Horn Basin as well as the sheep in the canyon just south of them.

A week after they had arrived at their new camp, there were sheep, antelope, elk, and even a buffalo hanging from poles lashed between cottonwoods just south of the hot springs. The weather was cold enough to keep the meat frozen so for now there was no need to dry any of it. Zach smiled every time he rode passed the warm pools next to the river, for there were naked bodies soaking in the warm mineral water constantly. He had watched Red Hawk and Meadowlark daily sneak off to the pools where they would disappear into the heavy mist coming off the water into the frigid air.

Zach and his wives had been in the pool several times as well, along with Star and the now nearly two-month-old twins. The warm healing waters made them forget, at least while they were in the pool, that the cold maker still had a firm grip on the land.

The new moon came again, isha-mea', the coyote moon, February, and still Red Hawk had not approached Wind in His Face. It was becoming almost comical, it seemed, that Meadowlark and Red Hawk were the only ones in the village that still thought their relationship was a secret. Finally, upon Red Hawks return from the warm pool late one afternoon Buffalo Heart said, "Red Hawk, are you going to continue to let the whole village laugh at you? You and Meadowlark must be blind and deaf not to be able to see or hear that everyone in the village knows what you two are doing, and yes Wind in His Face and Basket Maker knows too." Red Hawk was speechless, he was indeed so blinded by his desire for her that he had no idea everyone in the village was talking about them. At first he was embarrassed by Buffalo Hearts words, then a flash of anger that his friend hadn't said something before now.

Red Hawk couldn't answer his own question. Why he hadn't offered Wind in His Face the horses as he had planned when they first arrived? He looked at Buffalo Heart with disbelief in his eyes. Buffalo Heart knew he had embarrassed his friend and said, "I am sorry my brother, but I thought you knew, that is until it became obvious a couple of days ago you did not."

"What are the people saying about us?" Red Hawk asked.

"Everyone likes the match; Wind in His Face would have stopped it long ago if he didn't approve."

When Wind in His Face stepped from his lodge the next morning, he met Red Hawk standing in front of his lodge holding his five best horses by their lead ropes. Wind in His Face stood and tried to act surprised as he asked, "What is this?" with a very stern look on his face. The first thing to go through Red Hawk's mind was Buffalo Heart had tricked him, that Wind in His Face knew nothing of this. Wind in His Face enjoyed watching Red Hawk squirm, standing before him.

Red Hawk at this point was not going to be denied. He stood proud as he said, "I have come to give you my five best horses for Meadowlark to become my wife."

Meadowlark and Basket Maker were just inside the door flap. Meadowlark's breathing was fast and shallow as she listened to the words of her father and her lover.

Wind in His Hair just stood there silent as he watched this proud young man standing before him. He would have gladly taken just one horse, knowing Meadowlark would be well cared for with Red Hawk. However after several minutes he said, "You think these five horses is enough for a girl like Meadowlark?"

Before Red Hawk could answer Meadowlark burst from the teepee and jumped into Red Hawk's arms. Basket Maker was right behind her and stood next to her husband as they both smiled at their daughter. Wind in His Hair stepped forward and took the lead ropes of the five horses telling everyone in the village there would soon be a marriage celebration.

Chapter 18

The Buffalo Jump

EVERYONE IN THE village was excited about the marriage; it was a time of great celebration. Raven Wing, their new Shaman, had proven to have powerful medicine and no one in the village, even the elders could remember a winter when food was so plentiful.

Sun Flower and Shining Star had given Meadowlark and Basket Maker several soft tanned antelope skins for them to make Meadowlark's dress from. Shining Star and Little Dove were dying porcupine quills and using glass beads they had brought from Saint Louis, making the decorations for it.

While the women were preparing for the marriage of Red Hawk and Meadowlark, the men planned a buffalo hunt. The buffalo herd that was on the land near the river had moved away after the village was set up at the hot springs but they had been watched, and they were still within a half day's ride of the village. Everyone wanted fresh buffalo for the celebration of the two young lovers.

Buffalo Heart had mixed feelings. He was glad for his friend Red Hawk, Meadowlark was a lovely girl, but he already felt lonely. He watched the women sewing hides together for a new teepee and knew it wouldn't be long before he would be in their small teepee alone. Would he ever find a girl, he wondered. He thought about all the young women in the village and realized he would have to visit other villages if he was going to find a wife.

The day of the hunt dawned cold and gray. The clouds weren't threatening as they rode east toward the distant Big Horn Mountains, but they all knew that could change mighty fast. Ten hunters had left well before first light; Zach, Running Wolf and Jimbo was out in the lead with Grub and Ely close behind. Red Hawk, Buffalo Heart, and Benny had left even earlier than the rest. They were to find the herd and meet the other hunters at the base of Bull Mountain nearly twenty-five miles east of the village.

The hunters weren't traveling as fast as Zach wanted to. They were leading eight pack horses and four of them were pulling travoises to carry the anticipated meat and hides back to the village.

A cold breeze was blowing out of the north and the few inches of snow was crusty and crunched as the hooves of the horses broke through. They had been on the move for three hours heading toward the distant hill. Bull Mountain was just a hill standing only two or three hundred feet above the surrounding prairie. Three days before, the herd had been seen by High Back Bull and Standing Deer as they were hunting antelope.

This was new country for Zach and Running Wolf; neither of them had been out this way before. The Big Horn basin seemed to be full of game this winter, and Zach, like everyone else in the village, had never been able to hunt fresh meat all winter long. He knew they were riding ever closer to Cheyenne country. He remembered the cold, long winter just a couple of years ago when he had traveled for days in the bitter cold alone to find meat for his family, and the Cheyenne he'd had to fight to keep it. His eyes scanned the horizon for any sign of their enemies. He knew they could be hunting as well for this was the starving time of year for most tribes.

Benny, Red Hawk, and Buffalo Heart found the herd of buffalo, or at least part of it. On the plains just south west of

146

Bull Mountain there were nearly a hundred of the big hump back beasts. Red Hawk and Buffalo Heart both looked the land over very thoroughly and only a mile from where the buffalo were grazing was a gradual rise leading up to a steep rocky ledge with nearly a fifty-foot drop into large broken boulders. They both knew this was an ideal place to drive the unsuspecting animals over the cliff.

Red Hawk rode hard to intercept Grizzly Killer and the others. He needed several of them to move onto the ridge to the south and form a line at the top of the ledge to drive the buffalo over the cliff and into the rocks below.

He met up with Zach and the others only three or four miles west of their destination. After telling them of the plan, everyone was excited. From the time of their Grandfather's Grandfathers, the people had been hunting buffalo this way whenever the opportunity presented itself. Buffalo hunting is dangerous no matter how it is done, but stampeding the big animals, some weighting twice as much as the horses they ride, was much safer than riding in among them with their bows and lances.

Zach nor any of his white friends had ever taken part in a buffalo jump, but Grub and Ely had witnessed the aftermath of one years before while visiting a Crow village just south of the Yellowstone. It had been a gruesome sight with over fifty of the big animals lying below the jump. Although neither Grub nor Ely was anxious for this type of hunt, they all knew this was by far the safest way for them to take the needed meat.

Two hours later they were all in position. Their goal was to split the herd and stampede only a small portion of them over the cliff. They had all taken off their coats to wave over their heads to frighten the buffalo into a blind stampede. Their plan worked flawlessly. As they rode into the grazing animals screaming their war cries, the herd split with about thirty running up toward the cliff.

Jimbo was running alongside Ol' Red right behind the stampeding herd. He was barking and getting close enough to nip at their heels. For the big dog, this was the most fun he'd had in a long time.

It took only a couple of minutes for the lead buffalo to reach where the posted hunters would change their direction, pushing them over the jump. They too started screaming their war cries and waving their coats. The frightened buffalo turned just as expected. Red Elk was out on the edge as Zach and the others pushed the herd from behind, but in his excitement he had ridden on ahead of the others and was alongside the stampeding buffalo rather than behind it when they turned. As the massive beasts turned blindly running over the cliff, Red Elk and his horse was pushed over the edge along with the buffalo.

Once the leaders had jumped over the edge, High Back Bull and the others forming the picket line above split, allowing some animals through. When it was all over there were twenty of the big animals lying in a huge pile in the rocks at the bottom. Some were dead, some with broken legs that would have to be finished off. Some of the ones that were still alive were bellowing in obvious pain while others silently awaited their inevitable death.

No one had seen Red Elk being pushed over the edge and no one noticed he wasn't with them as they swiftly rode back down around the cliff to put the wounded animals out of their misery. It was Buffalo Heart that first saw the dead horse lying under a big buffalo bull that weighed nearly a ton, the bull being just as dead as the horse. Then just a few feet above them was Red Elk, his body crumpled and broken lying at the base of one of the boulders.

Shots were being fired all around them as the broken and wounded animal were put down. Buffalo Heart stood above his friend just staring, knowing Red Elk was dead but not wanting to believe it. This was supposed to be a safer way to hunt, but they had still lost one of their own.

Zach looked at the bloody mangled pile of buffalo before him. This was the easiest and fastest way he had ever witnessed in taking that many of the big animals, but the site sickened him at the same time. The broken legs, the painful bellowing, although he completely understood hunting in this fashion, he didn't like it, not at all.

Buffalo Heart knelt down and pulled Red Elk's broken body away from the boulder. It was then that Benny saw him and he shouted to the rest of them. Within moments they were all standing there with Buffalo Heart staring in disbelief at their dead friend.

The loss of Red Elk took the joy of a successful hunt from all of them. High Back Bull especially for now he had lost two of his friends through this season when the cold maker held the land in its grip.

They put Red Elk's body on one of the travois and had High Back Bull take him back to the village. They had killed many more buffalo than they could carry and High Back Bull would send more help and pack horses. They would not let the most valuable resource, the buffalo, go to waste.

The thick winter coats of the buffalo would make very warm robes, nearly as warm as the thick grizzly hide that Zach and his wives slept under during the cold months. Their tongues, hearts, and livers were a delicacy; their horns and bones made tools, from sewing awls to shovels to eating utensils. No parts of the big animal was wasted; the buffalo was the life blood of all the plains tribes and all tribes within traveling distance to the land of the buffalo.

They had planned on being back in the village that night but the skinning and butchering of that many large animals took the rest of the day. They built up a fire and used the green hides as sleeping robes. Zach figured it would take until midmorning at least to finish caring for all the meat. As the sun rose the next morning, Zach sent Jimbo on the big circular scout of the surrounding area, making sure none of their enemies had moved in.

High Back Bull returned with three more men and four women, each one of them leading a pack horse and a horse pulling a travois just a couple of hours after full light. Jimbo had returned and with the wag of his tail to let Zach know all was clear.

The green hides were lashed to the travois and as the buffalo were quartered they were stacked on the hides. By early afternoon they were headed back, all the travoises and packs horses loaded. They were carrying thousands of pounds of meat; enough for the marriage feast and to last the village until the sun finally pushed the cold maker back to the north, away from their land.

The burial of Red Elk was another sad affair for the village. Too many times over the years they had buried their young men as they hunted the life-giving buffalo. As their Shaman, Raven Wing spoke at the grave. She told them, "Red Elk gave his life so the people could live and no warrior ever had more honor than that. Just like everyone must be born to make their journey through this world, everyone must die to continue their journey into the land beyond, and Red Elk is making this journey with honor." She continued, "There will be a bright star streaking across the great trail in the sky tonight as Red Elk and his horse make the great journey."

Five days later the mood in the village was one of great anticipation and joy. It was the day Red Hawk and Meadowlark would be joined in marriage. This was the first time Raven Wing had done such a thing, and she prepared simply by remembering the many times she had watched Blue Fox as a young girl.

The ceremony was simple, just the taking of one another's hands and acknowledging they each accepted the other. A marriage always meant the village was growing and healthy, that a new generation of the Shoshone people would assure their future in the world.

Large buffalo roasts were put over the fires early in the morning. The tongues, hearts, and livers were put in the black iron pots that they had traded for at the Rendezvous. Zach, Running Wolf, and Benny just watched as their wives all went to help Basket Maker prepare Meadowlark for the ceremony.

Red Hawk had noticed Buffalo Heart was quieter than normal and had been the last couple of days. As Buffalo Heart was helping his friend dress in his finest, and setting a fan of the red feathers of a red tail hawk in Red Hawk's hair, Red Hawk asked, "What is it, Buffalo Heart. You have not spoken many words the last few days?"

Buffalo Heart didn't know how to answer his friend. He didn't know how to explain how happy he was for Red Hawk but yet how sad he felt inside. He knew he wasn't losing his friend, but that is what he was feeling. After a long pause, he said, "Red Hawk, I think I am envious of you and Meadowlark. I am so happy for you, but I will miss you as well."

Red Hawk choose his words carefully as he answered his lifelong friend, "I am only moving into a new lodge, my friend. We have been best friends all of our lives and that will not change, we will be friends until death." Buffalo Heart, smiled knowing his friend was right, they would always be friends, but he also knew their friendship, although strong, would be forever changed after today.

The ceremony took place midafternoon. Meadowlark was stunning in her beautifully decorated dress with bright red trade cloth ribbons tied into her hair. It had snowed the night before and most of the dirty trampled ground in the village was covered with a fresh coating of clean white snow. The air was cold, but the sun was shining bright with its warming rays warming both their skin and hearts. Everyone was enjoying themselves this day.

Of the many gifts given to help the couple to start their lives together, the most precious, especially to Red Hawk, was one of the great Medicine Dogs puppies. Running Wolf and Zach gave away two of the rapidly growing puppies that day. They gave Red Hawk first pick and Buffalo Heart the second. They both picked males, pups they both hoped would have the same great medicine as their father.

The next day Running Wolf offered Otter one or two of the pups to replace the dogs he had lost to the great bear late last fall. He was thrilled and picked the two females, thinking he could breed them to his older hound and even make better hunting dogs than he had now. The smallest of the litter was one of the little females and she had almost no gray in her. Otter called her White Wolf after her mother, the other female had more of her father's coloration and he called her Medicine Girl. He was hoping the name would help give her some of her father's powerful medicine.

The days were getting longer as the sun moved further north. Although the nights were still very cold, the sun was making the afternoons pleasant. Isha-mea', the coyote moon, gave way to yu'a-mea', the warming moon, and as March moved in, Zach had started thinking more and more about their home on Black's Fork over two hundred miles to the southwest.

It had been nearly a year since they had followed the trail down Black's Fork, and then across the Seeds-Kee-Dee and dry baron planes to the pass over the south end of the Wind River Mountains on their way to Saint Louis. That trip had been long and difficult but it had shown his family and friends what he had wanted them to see. The western expansion of America would eventually affect the Shoshone and Utes along with all the tribes of the west just as it had done with the Cherokee and Shawnee in his home in Kentucky.

Zach missed his home. He longed to be looking up at the towering peaks of the Uintah Mountains, the big meadow where their horse herd stayed and the dozens of familiar creeks full of beaver all across the north slope of the Uintah's.

Zach still had not given the twins their names. In his mind he thought he knew what their names were going to be, but, for some reason he did not understand, he had waited. They were now nearly four months old and growing unbelievably fast. One day in mid-March while he, Ol' Red, and Jimbo were out riding, a strong feeling came over him, and he saw his father sitting by a fire, an old beat up coffee cup in his hand. He felt a tear run down his cheek as he remembered all the mornings the two of them had sat by a fire just like what he was seeing, drinking coffee and planning their day.

In this vision his father never said a word; in fact he didn't even acknowledge Zach at all, but when Zach blinked, the vision was gone. He knew his father was telling him it was time to make his plans for the immediate future and first on that list was giving his twins their names.

He rode back to the village with a purpose. He stepped off Ol' Red and he and Jimbo both stepped into the lodge. He picked up Star and swung her around then dropped to his knees and kissed each of the twins. Then with a smile he looked at both of his wives and said, "Prepare for a feast, for tonight the little ones will be given their names.

Chapter 19

The Valley of the Wind River

THE NAMING CEREMONY was another joyful event for the village, everyone was there as Zach held his baby girl up, announcing to the world she would be known as Little Moon. Sun Flower remembered the night just before she had given birth when the moon, being only a small crescent, had shown through the clouds. It had been her standing next to Zach that had called it the little moon.

Zach handed the squirming baby back to her mother and picked up his baby boy. He repeated the process once more, announcing the baby boy would be called Jack after his grandfather. There was some disappointment with a few of the villagers who thought he should be given an Indian name like his sister had, but even those thought that being named after his grandfather was appropriate.

Jimbo's pups were growing even faster than the twins were. At almost four months they were nearly as large as most of the other dogs of the village. Buffalo Heart had named his pup, Little Bear, and since Red Hawk and Meadowlark had now moved into their new teepee together, Little Bear had become Buffalo Heart's constant companion and the pup had taken to his new friend just as rapidly as Jimbo had taken to Zach those years ago.

Red Hawk had named his pup Medicine Wolf, and the rapidly growing pup became an instant part of Red Hawk and Meadowlark's lodge. In fact, Medicine Wolf already had a protective nature and would growl at anyone that tried to enter their lodge.

Of the two remaining pups, they gave one to Benny and Little Dove, and then offered the last to Grub and Ely. Neither of these older trappers had ever had a dog, not since they had left home as teenagers. Neither of them felt they had the patience to train the pup like Jimbo was trained but both figured having another loyal companion with better eyes and ears than their own was a good thing. It didn't take long for both men to grow to love the large pups. Watching theirs and Benny's pups playing together gave them more pleasure than they ever thought was possible. Benny's pup had the most gray of all of them, nearly appearing blue in the sunlight, so Benny called him Blue. Ely thought back to his Pa's old hound dog named Charley that protected their homestead when he was a boy and with a nod of Grub's head their pup became Charley Two.

Benny, Red Hawk, and Buffalo Heart all listened to Zach and watched him closely with his interactions with the great medicine dog. All three of them had seen Jimbo in action many times over the years. Their goal was to have the great dog's pups' medicine as strong as their father's and they all believed they could be. Zach had told them many times that for that to happen, it was up to them as much as it was the dogs. Zach told them the more time they were willing to spend teaching the pups, as well as showing the pups their love, the more the pups would want to learn and please them.

Zach and Running Wolf enjoyed watching the boys working with their puppies several times each day. Both one on one with them and as a group. He would take Jimbo with them as a group and with Jimbo as their leader he was helping them learn to follow the simple hand signals. It wasn't long before Zach could see that with Jimbo leading these three growing pups they were a force to be reckoned with, by either man or beast.

They had taken Jimbo and the pups west into the Owl Creek Mountains. Grub, Ely, and Running Wolf had joined them to check out trapping possibilities for the spring season. They found several good creeks feeding Owl Creek itself and they all figured with the weather the way it was they needed to be out trapping.

Upon their return to the village, Spotted Elk and Charging Bull was waiting for them. They learned immediately that it was time to move the village back to the valley of the Wind River. High Back Bull and others that had been hunting far to the northeast had seen a large number of Cheyenne and Sioux moving this direction.

All of the tribes used the hot springs from time to time, and it had been an understanding since the time of their grandfathers that no tribe claimed them for their own. This was the reason Charging Bull's village had never wintered here before and they wouldn't have this year if Raven Wing had not told them it would be fine.

Everyone in the village believed it was her power that had kept their enemies away from the hot springs all winter. But now they all knew it was time to go back to their own land. They had stayed here longer than anyone thought they would. This had been a most bountiful winter, the first in many where there had been no hunger, so they had stayed on as the weather warmed. Charging Bull and Spotted Elk both knew if they met the Cheyenne or Sioux there would be no keeping the young warriors on both sides from a deadly battle. Not even the young warriors wanting to prove themselves in battle wanted to meet their enemies with women and children here.

Even before Charging Bull had finished telling Zach of their decision, lodges were coming down throughout the village. Zach had spent a lot of time exploring this new country whenever the weather allowed though out the winter. He told Charging Bull of a route they could take that he believed they could make better time and would be safer than having to chance fighting a battle in the steep narrow canyon of the Wind River.

Their Chief knew of the route but was concerned about a couple of places where the trail drops off the rugged breaks down into the Valley of their home. Zach told him that he would go with the young men pushing the horses and they would make the trail wide enough for the travoises to navigate by the time the rest of the village reached there. Charging Bull was in deep thought as he looked at Spotted Elk. Spotted Elk then said, "My Chief, I will take a half dozen of my best warriors and follow along behind to stop any attack that might come. It will be much easier to defend the village if we can move around and not be stuck in that canyon."

With a nod from Charging Bull the plan was set in place and within just a couple of hours the village was on the move. Jack and Little Moon were once again put in their cradle boards to ride one on each side of their mother's horse. Star and Gray Wolf rode setting astride in front of their mothers with all of the belongings of the families on travoises and pack horses.

By late afternoon, the villagers were a couple of miles east of the canyon and over halfway through the length of it. Grub and Ely had stayed with the village, watching over the women and children while Zach, Running Wolf, and Benny went with all the young men driving the horses. They had reached the first of the steep narrow drop offs where the trail starts off the top of the plateau. They slowed the horses down with Zach riding Ol' Red leading the way. The sure-footed mule had no trouble at all as Zach made his way down the steep slope. He made long switch backs down the quarter mile long slope and just as he had hoped, by the time the over three hundred horses had reached the bottom, they had pounded a fairly flat trail that zig zagged its way to the bottom. The trail wasn't wide enough in most places for the travois to drag level, but they all figured they could make it down the slope just fine.

Charging Bull kept the village moving until sunset, when they had reached the top of that first steep slope. Zach and the horse herd was nearly five miles in front of them. They would have been further, but they'd had to stop and dig out a couple of large boulders as they climbed out of the second of the steep draws leading off the plateau down to the river. The boulders were too close together for the travoises to go between.

Spotted Elk had left two experienced warriors nearly five miles behind the village as guards. He didn't believe they had anything to worry about, but just in case the Sioux and Cheyenne had any advance scouts out he wanted to know about it.

The next morning, Sun Flower, Shining Star, and Raven Wing all tied their pack horses, including the ones pulling their travoises together, and was the first to head down the switch backs Zach had made with the horses of that first slope on foot. This was the steepest and most dangerous place of any they had to navigate. When the entire village had made it safely to the bottom, Charging Bull followed, thankful for Grizzly Killer's suggestion that they come this way. Another hour on the trail and they were looking out over the valley of the Wind River; the valley that had been their home since the time of their grandfather's grandfathers.

Charging Bull had given much thought to where they would locate the village through the warm moons of the year. That night he came to Raven Wing to get her blessing on an area they had not used in many summers. It was nearly twenty-five miles further up the Wind River from their traditional places that were much closer to where the Popo Agie flows into it. Raven Wing, like everyone else in the village, had never questioned Charging Bull's decisions. She knew he always had the good of the people in mind and told him that she fully supported his decision.

Now they were back in the valley of the Wind River. Zach, Running Wolf, and Benny had left the horse herd and were back riding with their families. Star was high above the ground riding on Zach's shoulders as they continued following the river upstream.

Here on the valley floor, the only snow left from the cold winter was in the shade of the cottonwoods along the river, but it was melting rapidly under the warm afternoon sun. They still had over twenty miles to go when they stopped for their last night on the trail. With an early start the next morning, they would be setting up the village once again by sunset tomorrow.

The river was running higher than it had been all winter and was not as clear now. The snow melting from the lower slopes was carrying mud and silt into the river with it. Zach figured it would be another couple of months before the runoff was at its peak. By then the river would be full to the top of its banks and treacherous to cross. He hoped he would be back on the banks of Black's Fork long before then. In fact, he hoped to be on the trail heading home within the next couple of weeks.

Without the village being in the valley all winter, the game had returned to their traditional winter range, and they saw elk, deer, and sheep along the slopes just above the valley. Deer was plentiful in the willows along the river as they headed north toward the area Charging Bull had designated as the site for their village.

Golden eagles and many different hawks soared overhead, while Jimbo, Luna, and their pups checked out each and every bush along the way. Luna was still teaching her pups to hunt and Zach and his family laughed until their sides hurt as they watched a cottontail rabbit escape over and over again from the pups.

Springtime was a time that made Zach remember his childhood in Kentucky. It was April, and he knew the Dogwood would be in bloom. Here it would be at least another month before the trees even started to get their leaves. The white blossoms of the chokecherry and serviceberries was still six or seven weeks away, but the buds had swollen on the red willow along the creeks and he knew it wouldn't be long before the leaves started to sprout.

The sun had just disappeared behind the peaks to the west as they reached the large flat area on the west side of the river that would be home to the village. Zach and Running Wolf moved off to the western edge of the clearing, knowing their time here would be short. Everyone pitched in and before full dark all of the lodges were up and fires were burning. Cottonwoods along the river and pine and aspen on the slopes would provide all of the firewood the village would need for months.

Like most springs since Zach had been in the mountains, supplies were running short. The cornmeal was gone and the flour nearly gone and it was so full of weevils no one really wanted to eat it any longer. They still had coffee beans but Zach didn't figure they would last until Rendezvous. He thought about the Rendezvous this summer, planned once again for the Willow Valley. For the trappers, it was a time of celebration, seeing friends for that one time each year, but most importantly it was a time to resupply for another year.

Zach, Running Wolf, and their friends had done no trapping since the fall and Zach was torn whether to spend much of the spring trapping season on the trail going back to Black's Fork or stay and trap the tributaries of the Wind River for another month. After discussing this with Running Wolf and their wives, they decided to stay for one more month. If they didn't, they would have less than half their normal take of plews.

The following day nearly all of the hunting age men in the village went out hunting. This had been the first winter that Zach had spent with an Indian village. The amount of meat it took to keep that many people fed amazed him. This had been the first time since he and his Pa came west when he really understood how people could starve, especially in late winter. He had heard some elders taking about this being the first winter in their memory when they hadn't had to butcher horses to keep the people fed. Most of them thought that was because of the vision of Raven Wing and that was only one reason no one in the village wanted to see her leave.

That next morning Spotted Elk and Otter left to cover their back trail. They wanted to make sure the Sioux and Cheyenne that had been sighted were not looking to make war with them.

After all, it was the Cheyenne that had come into their land late last fall for their horses.

Zach and Running Wolf took their traps with them although hunting was their main purpose for today. If they found a good stream to set the traps, they would do so.

Spotted Elk and Otter had ridden hard and by midafternoon they were back up on top of the plateau. They had shot a yearling sheep just before they reached the top so they would have fresh meat for the night. By sunset they were only a few miles south of the hot springs, and with no sign of anyone following or at the springs, they turned and went back to the switch backs. The two of them camped at the top of the first steep slope just as the village had done a couple of days before.

By midday of that first day back, the first hunters to return to the village had already brought in three sheep. Not long after that another group brought in a cow and yearling elk. Grub, Ely, and Benny had shot a large cow elk and two deer. They brought in the deer but needed a couple more horses for the elk.

Zach and Running Wolf had each taken an elk, but just like Grub, Ely, and Benny they would have to return the next morning with four pack horses to bring in that much meat. They had cut the hind quarter from one of them so their families would have fresh meat for tonight.

As the sun set, there was still one group of hunters that had not returned, although none of them had planned to be out overnight. Spotted Elk and Otter, in covering their back trail, wasn't expected back that night but everyone else was.

By morning, Charging Bull was forming a search party to go out and find the missing hunters. It was Stone Knife, Broken Nose, and Standing Deer that had not returned. Stone Knife and Broken Nose were brothers while Standing Deer was Stone Knife's son. They were all great warriors and experienced hunters. None of the three of them had a rifle; they all carried traditional bows with stone-tipped arrows and Stone Knife also carried a long deadly lance with a hand chipped stone point nearly six inches long tied to its tip with sinew covered with pine pitch.

Stone Knife's skill at knapping detailed points for his knives, lances and arrows had always been a source of great pride for him. The nearly razor sharp points made his arrows and lances extremely effective for penetrating the hair and thick hides of elk, moose, and bear.

Zach and Jimbo led the group of searchers in looking for the missing hunters, Benny had brought along his pup, Blue, and Grub had brought Charley Two, but until a good trail was found they kept the pups on leashes and neither of the excited young dogs liked being restrained. They were used to running free with Jimbo and they fought the leashes until both Benny and Grub were having second thoughts about bringing them.

Jimbo picked up the scent of the three missing hunters about five miles south of the village and within another mile, one of their horses was spotted. The animal was nervous and shied away from them. The dried lather caked to his flanks and neck told them he had run hard for a long distance. High Back Bull spoke, "That is Standing Deer's pony. I helped break him just last spring."

Ely studied the tracks, and it became clear to him that the horse was alone, his was the only set of tracks leading north toward the village while the tracks of all three of them had ridden south.

They finally caught the nervous animal and took it with them as they followed the tracks that turned west toward the mountains. Soon the tracks were mixed with those of about a dozen elk and it became obvious to them all three of the hunters were following the elk as they moved toward the timbered slopes of the mountain.

Chapter 20

Scent on the Wind

RAVEN WING HAD MIXED emotions about leaving. She felt needed here now that Blue Fox had gone to the world beyond. She loved their home on Black's Fork as much as Running Wolf and the rest of her family did and wanted to return there. It was never a matter of deciding, she would go with her husband. It didn't matter to her where he went, she would be by his side, but that didn't change the fact that she felt bad about leaving the people of the village where she had been born and raised.

Sun Flower knew her sister well and could see and even feel the conflict she felt. She too felt much the same even though she was not looked to as a healer and shaman like Raven Wing. She had enjoyed spending these last few moons so near her parents, brother, and his family, but she knew, just like Raven Wing did, that this was no longer their home. Their home was on Black's Fork.

Shining Star was not from this village. Being Ute, she had been raised with the Shoshone being her enemy, but she had never felt that way in this village. White Feather and Bear Heart treated her as their own daughter and she had grown to love them both, but she too longed to be back home. Although she and Running Wolf were from the village of Stands Tall on the south slope of the Uintah's, in her heart, being on the banks of Black's Fork looking out across the big meadow was home and that is where she longed to be.

It had been nearly a year since any of them had been there and the three of them, even with differing emotions, longed to go back.

*****

The trail wound in and out of willows and brush, through scattered stands of cottonwoods and aspen. The elk followed their own trail back to the protection of the timbered slopes of the mountain. A small creek fed by a spring started way up above them on the mountain. Normally only a foot wide with just a trickle of water, it was now nearly three feet wide and rushing down the little canyon that it had formed over countless thousands of years.

This was not the first time hunters from the village had followed this trail. In fact, Stone Knife and Broken Nose had headed directly for it when they left the village the morning before. They knew the area well, and they'd had success hunting up high on the mountain here many times in the past.

Although Ely was leading the way he didn't have to follow the tracks for Jimbo was out in front. All he was doing was following the big dog. Zach could tell Jimbo had their scent, and he didn't believe as long as the weather held it would take all that long to find out what had happened to them. The Wind River where the village set was nearly twenty miles from the mountains, but with Jimbo following the scent and moving at a fast trot they covered the twenty miles in just a couple of hours.

Ely stopped as the trail started up into the small canyon and got down to study the tracks. He could see plainly where the three horses had gone up but only the one coming back down. The one coming down had been running at what Ely figured was full out. There were tracks of a few deer on top of the horse tracks but the horse tracks were all on top of the tracks left by the elk. For whatever reason, the elk had not come down off the mountain last night or this morning.

As they started up, the trail led through pine then scattered aspen and sage flats. There was elk sign everywhere and they all could see the reason the hunters had come this way. They were only about a mile into the canyon when Jimbo stopped dead still in the trail, the hair standing up down the center of his back. Ely and Zach spotted the small black bear at the same time. It ran into the trees at the top of the clearing they were moving through. Ely turned around and said, "Just a two-year-old, first spring without its mama." Zach nodded, and they moved on.

They couldn't move nearly as fast on this mountain trail as they had down in the valley. As the trail twisted and turned through the trees and sage flats, the horses could only walk. It was a steady walk, and they were still making pretty good time. About two miles up the trail left the small creek, and they followed it diagonally up and over the ridge to the north. Once on top they stopped to study the area before them. Stretching out for well over a mile to the west was a grass covered park with a few scattered sage, but for the most part it was just the winter brown grass and dead wild flowers from last summer's growth. It would be at least another month before the grass started to turn green for this year.

The trail forked going in separate directions only fifty yards or so into the large meadow. The right fork slowly turned to the north and toward a heavy stand of dark timber. Ely stopped to once again examine the tracks even though he knew which way the hunters had gone just by watching Jimbo. Grub and Benny now released Blue and Charley Two; both pups immediately ran up, wanting to play with their father. Jimbo knew this was not a time for play and let both pups know with a growl that he was not to be bothered.

Like Jimbo, the pups could smell all of the different scents in the air and coming off the ground; they just didn't understand which scent they were supposed to follow. The trail had been heavily used by elk and sheep for generations and had

165

been pounded down in places six inches deep. There were some deer tracks but the main use was by the elk and sheep.

A slight breeze had started blowing from the west down the mountain. Zach watched Jimbo with his head held high, testing the breeze. He noticed the hair start to raise on his neck. Although the movement of the hair was nearly imperceptible, he and Running Wolf both noticed. They both knew the big dog well enough to see the slight change. The pups had their noses to the ground, trying to separate each of the distinct scents they could smell, neither knowing which animal each scent belonged to.

Zach looked ahead into the breeze as Running Wolf rode up beside him, he too had seen the slight movement on Jimbo's neck, and asked, "Grizzly Killer, what do you think he smells?"

"Don't know, but there's somethin' on the breeze he don't like. It ain't very strong but it is there." Ely and Grub both heard what the two of them had said and Ely looked back at them with a puzzled look. He had not seen anything from Jimbo except him sniffing the air. Ely had watched the communication between Zach and Jimbo a few times before and completely understood why the Indians believed the two could talk to one another. He knew they didn't talk but truly wondered if they could read each other's thoughts. How else did Zach and Running Wolf both know there was something on the breeze that the big dog didn't like? He was closer to Jimbo than either of them were and he hadn't seen a thing.

A soft low growl started from deep in Jimbo's throat and the two pups both raised their heads. Ely could tell the two pups were paying very close attention to their father. Zach whistled softly and Jimbo looked at him, every muscle in the big dog was tense. Zach moved his hand into the breeze and then in a half circle and without hesitation Jimbo took off with both pups right on his heels.

Ely looked back at Zach and asked, "You have any notion 'bout what's up there?"

"No, but whatever it is Jimbo don't like it none. Could be Blackfeet, Crow, or some critter, but if it is a critter it ain't a deer, elk, or sheep. He don't act that way when he smells them. We best stay right here 'til Jimbo gets back."

Ely nodded but Grub said, "Y'all knows we's goin' be spendin' the night up here, don't ya. We ain't no way gonna make it back today." They all nodded, now more worried than ever about the missing men.

It was about fifteen minutes later when Zach could see Jimbo running at full speed back to them. The pups were trying to keep up but we're getting further behind Jimbo with each stride of his long muscular legs. Zach said, to no one in particular, "He found somethin'. He wouldn't be movin' like that if'n he didn't have somethin' to tell me."

Jimbo came running in and stopped right in front of Zach. He growled and then barked once, turned and started running back in the direction he had just come, expecting Zach to follow right behind him.

Zach didn't hesitate, and neither did the rest. The pups had just reached the group when everyone kicked their mounts into a dead run trying to catch the great medicine dog. They ran hard for over a mile across this long wide park. Jimbo slowed as he approached the quakies at its western edge. Two golden eagles took flight from the ground right at the edge of the trees. Zach and the rest knew something was dead, or the eagles wouldn't have been on the ground.

Ely, still in the lead, approached with caution. Everyone had their weapons ready as they got close. Then the carcass of a large elk came into view. There had been wolves at it during the night or maybe even earlier today, but the two arrows sticking in its side were still there.

High Back Bull said, "Those arrows are Standing Deer and Stone Knife's." Ely and Grub both dismounted and studied the tracks around the downed elk. They could tell it had been shot back in the trees by at least one of the arrows and ran out here before either being shot again or succumbing to its wounds. They found no moccasin tracks at all, The ground had been thoroughly torn up by four or five wolves feeding on the carcass and neither Ely nor Grub thought the hunters had approached their kill.

Why hadn't they followed their wounded elk? That was the question the searchers tried to answer as they carefully studied the ground and area back in the aspens from where the elk had run. It was plain to see this elk had been in a herd when Stone Knife and Standing Deer had hit it with their arrows.

Running Wolf found the tracks where the hunters had ambushed the unsuspecting elk, nearly a quarter mile back into the trees. A few minutes later, Jimbo gave a single bark, He had smelled drops of blood where another elk had been wounded. They figured that Broken Nose had hit another in the herd and the three of them had followed the other one.

The elk had all scattered when the hunters had surprised them, making the blood trail the only way to track him and he was bleeding very little. Ely finally found where he believed the three men had stepped, breaking the dry grass with their smooth soled moccasins. It was Zach that found the next blood drops giving them a direction to look ahead for more signs of the trail.

The wounded elk was heading down a gradual slope through the aspen forest, but now the sun was setting and they knew this search would have to wait until morning. They set up for the night right there in the protection of the trees and High Back Bull and Benny went back to the elk carcass and cut off enough meat for their evening meal and for morning. They knew wolves or bears would likely be back to the carcass in the night and there may be nothing left of it by morning.

By the time they crawled under their bed rolls for the night, the gentle breeze that had been blowing most of the day from the west shifted. It was now coming from the south and gaining in strength. By midnight it was gusting hard, and they all knew a storm was on its way.

The south wind was warmer than what had been blowing throughout the day but this far up on the mountain it was still cold. Zach pulled his buffalo robe tight around him trying to keep the wind from getting under it as Jimbo lay curled up at his feet. He knew if they didn't find the missing hunters before the storm covered all sign of them they may never find them or know what had happened to them. He thought about how easy Jimbo had followed their trail through most of the day, but the breeze had picked up in the afternoon and he had lost the scent. Now with the wind blowing hard he didn't figure Jimbo would be able to follow a scent trail at all.

Zach hadn't realized he had even dozed off when suddenly he was awakened by wolves howling right next to him. Blue and Charley Two were both sitting on their haunches with noses in the air howling into the dark night sky. There howls were answered by wolves less than a half mile away. Jimbo had never howled with the wolves, but Luna, their mother, was pure wolf and she had howled ever since Zach and Jimbo had rescued her as a tiny pup.

Jimbo was standing up still at Zach's feet, staring out into the darkness toward the howling wolves. He and the pups had heard the wolves fighting over the carcass of the dead elk. Everyone was awake as they listened to the haunting howls carried on the wind through the cold night air.

The sky was dark as Zach looked up to check the time. The big dipper circling the north star had been his night time clock ever since his Pa had first showed him how it moved when he was just a boy. It was gone, covered by the layer of clouds that the wind had ushered in. The south wind always seemed to bring storms with it. Zach knew the wind would shift before the actual storm reached them. As long as the wind came from the south he figured they still had time to find the missing hunters.

Morning dawned with the south wind gusting just had it had through the night. The wind blowing through the bare branches of the quakies reminded Zach of a woman moaning, mourning for a lost loved one. He hoped it wasn't the wind mourning for the lost hunters.

Zach had a fire going before it was light enough to see the trail, and by the time it was light they had all eaten their fill of the elk. The wounded elk they were tracking was not bleeding on the outside enough to leave a good trail, the blood drops were few and far apart. After they had found a few drops, a direction of travel could be seen and it became much easier to follow after that.

There were no horse tracks along this trail and Zach figured they had to have left their horses somewhere up above before stalking the elk and subsequently following the wounded ones trail. He and Running Wolf turned back, knowing Ely would find the elk and hopefully the hunters. He wanted to know what had happened to the horses. What had spooked the one they had found to run hard all the way off the mountain?

An hour later, Zach and Running Wolf were slowly covering the ground well above where the hunters had shot the elk. They were both watching Jimbo as much as the ground around them. They had spread out to cover a larger area. When Jimbo stopped, Zach watched and then Running Wolf noticed the big dog with his nose high into the wind. The hair starting to stand up the full length of his back.

Zach checked the prime under the frizzen of his Hawken and then glanced over to Running Wolf as he was doing the same. What was up ahead? Was it an enemy waiting in ambush? Was it the wolves from last night or a bear like the one they had seen coming up here? Zach's eyes were straining to see through the trees. A couple of minutes passed that seemed like hours, then Jimbo started forward once again, this time at a very slow walk.

Chapter 21

Like Demons from Within the Mountain

BY THE TIME the light had started to fade after the sun had set the night before, Sun Flower and Shining Star knew Grizzly Killer and the others would not return for the night. Sun Flower suckled Jack and then Little Moon. She did not understand why, but since the babies were a couple of months old, she was producing more milk and was able to provide all that the growing infants wanted. The women knew Grizzly Killer and Running Wolf were great warriors and with Jimbo with them there was none better anywhere, but as they looked at the mountains to the west they were worried, yet they didn't know why.

Raven Wing with Gray Wolf in her arms joined them, she too had a worried expression on her face. She didn't say anything to her sisters, but she'd had a dream just before dawn. A dream that had kept her awake ever since. In it she had seen a great grizzly bear attacking horses, she didn't know for sure whether the dream was about the past, future, or present and that worried her.

Although she hadn't seen the dead horses, she saw the great bear that had killed last fall. She had heard the stories about it many times, and how the bear towered over the horses when he stood up. She hoped with all her heart that those

171

stories were what had prompted the dream. In the dream the bear she saw did tower over the horses and with one powerful blow of the huge front paw, one of the horses collapsed to the ground and didn't move. That is when she woke up, her heart was racing and she was breathing hard, like she had been running. She sat up, seeing the dream time and time again in her mind.

She didn't want to worry Sun Flower and Shining Star any more than she knew they already were, so she said nothing to them or anyone else for now. Little Dove joined them and asked, "What do you think, Raven Wing, will our husbands be home today?"

Raven Wing answered without hesitation, "I do not believe we will see them today or even tomorrow."

Sun Flower looked at her sister now more worried than ever and asked, "What do you know, Raven Wing? What is it you have seen?"

Raven Wing knew she had said too much; Sun Flower knew her too well. Sun Flower was always the bold outspoken one of the two and had been since they were little, and she knew she couldn't lie to her even if she wanted to. They all stepped inside, out of the gusting wind, and she told them of her dream. They all listened, now more worried than before until Shining Star looked at Sun Flower and said, "Our husband did not get his name because the great bears killed him, and if he meets another one, there will be more claws to put on his necklace and Jimbo's collar." Sun Flower smiled knowing she was right, but they all still understood how dangerous a grizzly was and so many things could go wrong.

*****

Not being able to see anything in front of them, Zach watched Jimbo closely. A hundred yards ahead was a large spruce, standing alone in the forest of aspen. The wind, still gusting from the south, was carrying the scent Jimbo could smell.

The big dog continued moving forward very slowly. He glanced back once, checking on Zach even though he knew both he and Ol' Red would be right behind him. Zach watched the muscles ripple under Jimbo's thick fur and knew every one of the dog's senses were on high alert. Then Ol' Red shook his head, his ears steady and pointed right at the big spruce. Zach glanced over to Running Wolf and he too was concentrating on the area around and behind the tree.

Zach stopped and held his hand back for Running Wolf to do the same. They were just out of arrow range of the tree but not rifle range. Not being able to see through the spruce, he didn't want to walk into an ambush. He motioned for Running Wolf to stay while he turned, walking Ol' Red around the tree while not getting any closer to it.

He had only moved fifty yards to the right when he could see a horse lying on the ground behind the spruce. He watched for only a moment before knowing the horse was dead. Once again he studied the area all around them before motioning Running Wolf forward. They approached the dead horse from both sides of the spruce. Zach moved his hand in a circle over his head and Jimbo immediately left, scouting a full circle around them.

A rawhide braided lead rope was still tied to an aspen about five yards from the spruce. It had been that lead rope that had prevented the horse from fleeing. But what alarmed both Zach and Running Wolf was the deep gouges running down the horse's neck. Zach looked at the scars on the neck and shoulder of his beloved mule; he knew there was only one thing in the mountains that could have made those marks. The grizzly was back. It became evident to the two of them the other two horses had broken free from their pickets and Running Wolf followed their trail. It was only about a hundred yards when he found where the bear had caught one of the other fleeing horses.

It was a gruesome scene. The horse had been dragged down from behind; the five-inch claws digging deeply into the horse's rump. There had been quite a struggle as the horse fought to get away but the strength of the big bear and his weight overpowered the struggling horse. A bite through the horse spine finally stopped the fight. Running Wolf marveled at both the speed and power the bear had to be able to catch and kill the fleeing horse.

Jimbo came back, letting them know the area was clear. So without hesitation, they left to catch up with Grub, Ely, and the others.

Blue and Charley Two knew Jimbo was approaching long before any of the men did. They turned and ran back to meet him. The two pups were excited, but they were learning fast. Just from the way Jimbo carried himself they knew he was working and was not in a playful mood. Just minutes later Zach and Running Wolf trotted up to the others and let them know what they had found.

Benny asked, "Do ya figure, it's the same one that killed, Howling Dog?"

Zach looked at Ely and Grub before he nodded and said, "I don't figure there could be two grizzlies that big in this same area, and this is a big bear. The claw marks down the horse's neck, where the bear had broken it, were as wide as the scars on Ol' Red here, and boys, that bear took a dozen shots from me and Running Wolf's rifles and a dozen arrows before he stopped comin' at us."

Both High Back Bull and Benny had seen this bear last fall from across the glade as it stood behind the dead horses. Benny shuttered, and a chill ran down his back as he remembered the eerie feeling that morning, a few months ago. The question now on all of their minds was, after killing the horses did the grizzly follow Stone Knife, Broken Nose, and Standing Deer? Or had he left the area after the attack.

So far neither Ely, nor any of them, had seen any sign of the grizzly on the trail they were following, but Zach was troubled about the fact that neither of the dead horses had been eaten on. It appeared the bear had killed just for the thrill of killing; the same thing he had done last fall, that is, until it came to a man. The bear had eaten a good portion of Howling Dog before he abandoned the corpse on the small lake's shore.

He now feared more than ever what they might find ahead of them.

The wounded elk had stayed on a narrow game trail as he ran down the gentle slope away from the hunters. It was obvious to Ely that the hunters were in no hurry, not wanting the push the wounded animal further than it was going to go on his own.

They had gone another mile after Zach and Running Wolf had joined them when they could hear water cascading over rocks. A quarter mile further and the trail turned downhill following along the top of a deep rocky chasm.

As Zach looked over the edge to the creek over a hundred feet below, the water was white as it cascaded down the rocky gorge. The trail got much steeper as it followed the rim of the gorge toward the valley floor several miles to the east. Jimbo stopped. He was about fifty yards in front of Ely and Zach. Running Wolf, Benny, and the others were right behind them. Grub had moved off to the side several yards and was about even with Ely and Zach.

As Jimbo stopped, so did the men. All but Grub. He could see something that looked out of place just a few yards in front of him. There was a thick stand of pines just twenty yards to his right. He took a few more steps as Jimbo sniffed the air; all eyes were on the big dog. Blue and Charley Two was ten yards behind their father and they too were sniffing the scent in the air. They all watched as the hair started to stand down the center of their backs.

Grub took several steps forward and then he too stopped. His eyes instinctively covering the area all around them. The ground immediately before him was torn up from a very large bear that appeared to be charging directly to where Jimbo was standing. He called to Ely then double checked the prime on his long rifle. Zach was watching his dog as Running Wolf slowly moved over to the ledge and looked down at the roaring water of the creek below.

His heart sank as he saw the three bodies on the rocks below. There was no doubt it was the lost hunters. All three of them lay still, forever now in the land beyond. He called the others over. None of them said a word as sadness filled their hearts. Only a moment later Zach looked back at his dog. Jimbo's nose was on the ground and he knew the dogs would not have any trouble following the scent of the big bear.

Ely pieced together what had happened from the tracks and it was obvious the great grizzly had charged the three hunters while they were tracking the wounded elk. He had come at them from the cover of the dark pines at what appeared to be blinding speed. The hunters hadn't had a chance. There was no place for them to go except over the edge. It had either been that or face a thousand pounds of raging fury, with paws wider than a man's head and with enough power to break a horse's neck with one blow.

After the bear had chased the three men off the cliff, Ely good see how he had stood at the edge, looking down at where the three of them had disappeared over it.

Without warning a cold wind gust hit them from the north, and as they figured out a way to retrieve the bodies from nearly a hundred feet down the vertical rock face, the temperature dropped over ten degrees while they were tying all of their ropes together to lower one of them down to the bodies below.

Running Wolf, being the lightest of them, volunteered to be lowered down. He had just stepped over the edge after the rope was securely tied around him when a heavy snow started with the temperature falling even more. It took only five minutes for him to be lowered to the bottom and there was already snow starting to build up on the bodies, even at the bottom of this narrow chasm.

When he got close to the bodies, he could see they did not willingly jump. It did not matter how hopeless, all three of them had tried to fight the grizzly. Standing Deer had been hit with one of the massive paws, the bear's claws ripping into his side, and he was thrown off the cliff. The bears huge paw and deadly claws had come down on Stone Knife's head, with the claws nearly ripping his scalp and face off, it was a gruesome sight. Broken Nose still held a bloody knife in his right hand but his left arm was missing from the elbow down.

Running Wolf struggled to secure the rope around the stiff frozen body of Standing Deer then motioned for the men above to pull it up. They had tied the top end of the rope to Benny's saddle and led his horse through the trees until the body was back on top. It took nearly an hour to get the three bodies and then Running Wolf back up out of the gorge, and in that hour nearly three inches of snow had fallen.

It was now well into the afternoon but with the storm they really couldn't tell how much daylight was left, but they all knew they would never get off the mountain before dark. With the heavy snow and cloud cover, the light was fading fast.

They left the bodies laid out at the top of the gorge and retreated into the pines to spend a cold, miserable night with the falling snow and howling wind. With the wind changing, now coming from the north, the sound it made had changed as well. As it whipped through the barren aspen branches and across the rocky gorge, its moan changed to a lower pitch. It no longer sounded like a woman mourning as it had the night before. Now it sounded like demons from within the mountain were screaming and growling at them.

Zach could tell most of his Indian friends hated the eerie sound and none of them wanted to spend the night, but each of them knew they had no choice. They would just have to live with their superstitions and fears through the night until they could once again leave this place of death and the haunted moaning of the mountain and wait for the light a day.

Just like last fall in the glade and at the small lake they built multiple fires, not only for the cold but to keep the grizzly away as well. They didn't need to worry about who was going to stand watch; there wasn't one of them that was going to sleep this cold and miserable night.

Chapter 22

Sorrowful Return

GRIZZLY KILLER'S LODGE was full as the light faded. Sun Flower, Shining Star, Raven Wing, and Little Dove along with the four children were all inside. Spotted Elk and Otter had returned in the afternoon with the news that they didn't believe anyone was following them to their summer home. Still, the women's mood was solemn. Even the toddlers could tell their mothers were worried and just wanted to be held instead of their usual continuous play. Although the snow was light down in the valley along the banks of the Wind River, the temperature had fallen just as much as it had up on the mountain.

None of them could get the thought of Raven Wing's dream from their minds and they all had the same question, *"Was the killer grizzly back?"* With Star having crawled up on Sun Flower's lap and Gray Wolf on Raven Wing's, Shining Star and Little Dove was each holding a twin. With almost no conversation and the warmth from the small fire in the center of the lodge, it wasn't long before all of the children were asleep.

After darkness had fallen, the women all knew their husbands would not be back, and they all stayed right there in Grizzly Killer's lodge for the night. Sometime well after midnight they were awakened by a shrill scream from not far away. It was so loud all four women were instantly awake and sitting up. An instant later, dogs were barking and men were shouting. Shining Star added sticks to the fire and just another moment had passed when the door flap was thrown open as Spotted Elk put his head inside and asked, much louder than he intended to, "Are you alright?"

Sun Flower answered back, "Yes, what is it? What has happened?"

Spotted Elk said as he was turning to leave, "A bear, a bear has taken Flower Song." He then hurried away into the dark.

Within minutes the whole village was outside their teepees and fires were being started in the outside fire pits. Blossom, Flower Song's mother, could be heard crying uncontrollably as men from all over the village were preparing to leave in the dark snowy night.

With the outside fires getting started all around the village, the women could see more of what was going on. White feather was with Blossom, trying to calm her, but there was no calming the hysterical mother. Flower Song was just eleven summers, and she was Blossom and High Eagle's only child.

The snow was falling much heavier in the village now than it had been earlier and although no one thought the little girl had a chance of survival, every man there was willing to brave the dark stormy night to retrieve her.

Otter had his dogs, Tracker and the two half-wolf pups that were now nearly as heavy as Tracker, and he turned them loose as Spotted Elk, Otter, High Eagle and three others headed out following the bear. Tracker could be heard through the darkness telling everyone he was on a fresh scent. Otter could tell by the change in the dog's half bark, half howl if the trail he was following was fresh or old or when the dog treed its quarry. Jimbo's pups were more like the big medicine dog himself, silent as they ran but staying right with Tracker.

The bear, with one swipe of his massive paw, had torn through the heavy buffalo hide lodge covering making an opening eight feet high and going nearly to the ground. He had stepped through the opening and picked up the sleeping girl. Blossom had screamed but as High Eagle jumped up the entire lodge came down of top of them as the bear took out a half dozen of the lodge poles, carrying the child in his mouth as he left.

It was a dark dreary morning as the light slowly filtered through the thick layer of clouds and falling snow. The snow was now light, but it had already covered all sign of the bear's tracks. Even Tracker had lost the scent several times now and Otter had called him and the pups back. He was now following a scent again but Otter could tell the scent was so weak that Tracker was having a hard time following and he wasn't convinced that the scent the dogs were on was even that of the bear any longer.

*****

Zach and the other searchers had spent a long, cold night huddled between four fires they had kept going throughout the night. They were cold and tired and ready to leave. The wind had died down enough to stop the eerie moans, but all of the men were anxious to get their friends' bodies off the cold windy mountain. The sky was still dark and the clouds low but the snow had finally stopped.

They built a travois and tied it to Standing Deer's young horse. High Back Bull told them how proud Standing Deer had been of the colt and he would like that it was his horse that was carrying them back to the village.

As Zach tightened the cinch on his saddle and patted Ol' Red on the neck, he looked at the cold frozen bodies on the travois and thought about the village and the sorrow they were carrying with them. He thought about Laughing Woman and Singing Bird, the wives of Stone Knife and Broken Nose, how their laughter and singing had always brought happiness to the village. Sorrow filled his heart as he thought about the shock and sorrow their return would bring to them all. He had no way of knowing the killer bear had already brought more sorrow with the taking of young Flower Song.

Zach took the lead as the solemn procession headed out. Jimbo waited for Zach to point then he headed out with the two pups right on his heels. Standing Deer's horse was being led by High Back Bull. He sat proud on his horse, but everyone could see the sadness in his eyes. This was the second friend he had lost in the last few months, both of them to the killer bear.

High Back Bull had spent most of the night thinking about the giant grizzly. He could still see the bear standing on the far side of the glade last fall. He could see in his memory the mangled remains of Howling Dog, his boastful and arrogant friend. He looked back at the travois and thought about how different the village would be without Standing Deer, his father, and uncle.

High Back Bull had heard the stories of Grizzly Killer ever since he was a young teenager. The necklace with the nearly 5 inch claws that both he and the great medicine dog wore around their necks were made from bears he had killed by himself. Running Wolf, Grizzly Killer's Ute partner and the husband of their Shaman and healer, had faced the great bears alongside Grizzly Killer and he too had survived. With their help, he knew in his own heart they would stop the giant bear.

Zach didn't think they could make it back to the village before nightfall, but he was going to push as hard as he could and try. They had several miles of rugged mountain to cross before reaching the valley floor and another twenty miles across the valley to reach the village.

The sky was still dark, and the clouds were so low even the tops of the trees were shrouded in their foggy mist but the snow had stopped. They were pushing through nearly a foot of new snow as they followed the same trail back the way they had come. The wounded elk forgotten now the hunters had been recovered.

They came out at the top of the grass covered park not far from where Standing Deer and Stone Knife had killed the elk, and without delay continued down toward the valley floor. A herd of nearly two dozen elk standing just inside the tree line to the south of them stopped grazing and watched as the horses and riders rode through the mile-long park.

Zach watched Jimbo. He was not working as far ahead as he usually did. The big dog stopped and with him both pups. All three of them were watching the elk. Zach expected the pups to take off after them, but to his surprise they didn't. The pups stayed with their father and it appeared to him that both pups were paying a lot closer attention to their surroundings now than when they had started this search. He smiled, thinking Jimbo really was teaching them. They were nearly past the elk when the herd got nervous and bounded away into the aspen forest.

Even with the snow and pulling the travois, they were making good time, better than Zach had figured they could. Just before they reached the valley floor their progress slowed. Finding a pathway through the thick pines wide enough for the travois took extra time and care, but just before midday they came out of the forest and onto the grass and brush covered valley floor.

They stopped there to rest the horses for a little while and they all ate a piece or two of jerky. Zach was looking back up at the mountain, wondering where the grizzly would have gone. He thought about the grizzlies he had killed in the past, and only one of them had come in to bait. He did not believe it would do any good to try to bait this killer unless he himself was the bait. This bear seemed to prefer human flesh. He had passed on the dead elk and he'd killed many horses and so far had not eaten on any of them.

Grub, Ely, Benny, and Running Wolf all walked up to him and a moment later High Back Bull joined them. It was High Back Bull that spoke first, "Grizzly Killer, you have faced killer bears before." Zach just nodded at the young man. High Back Bull continued, "This bear has killed two of my friends, and two of our best warriors. I feel it is my duty to stop the bear, but I will need your help.

Ely put his hand on High Back Bull's shoulder. He could feel the pain the young man was in. Zach nodded at him, then said, "High Back Bull, this is as bad of a bear as I have ever seen. It will take all of us working together to stop this killer. He is smart, attacking when only he has the advantage. We must take that advantage away from him and with enough guns we will stop him.

"But how do we do that? How do we take away his advantage?" High Back Bull asked.

"I do not know yet. We will return to the village and honor our fallen warriors. We will council with Charging Bull, Spotted Elk, and the elders and together we will find a way." High Back Bull nodded, accepting what Grizzly Killer had said.

They continued on. Zach set a pace as fast as he believed the travois could handle and with nearly two hours of daylight left, they arrived at the village.

Zach noticed while they were still a half mile out all of the guards around the village, instinctively he knew something had happened there while they were gone. His first thought was the village had been attacked by the Sioux and Cheyenne that were heading toward the hot springs as they left there. He kicked Ol' Red into a run, worried now about his family.

Jimbo had beaten him to their lodge and while Zach and Running Wolf were still over a hundred yards away, the four women that had been together ever since their men had left all stepped out of the teepee. Jimbo ran to each one of them before Zach and Running Wolf got there. Benny was only a few yards behind.

Grub watched the happy reunion in front of them and he knew the joy was going to be short lived. For High Back Bull was leading the horse and travois and he was not far behind.

Spotted Elk and Otter were the first to meet them and went straight to the travois. Zach was still looking into the loving eyes of his wives when they heard an awful scream. It was the voice of Laughing Woman, screaming in anguish as she ran out and saw the bodies of her husband and son. Only a moment later another sobbing moan as Singing Bird met the travois as well.

High Back Bull had no words, he just sat there on his horse and the sadness he felt reflected on his face and in his eyes. Otter walked up and took the lead rope from him and simply nodded at the young man. He led Standing Deer's horse with the travois to the center of the village.

Charging Bull was waiting, a fire already burning. Although Flower Song's body had not been found, everyone knew the little girl was dead. They had followed the grizzly for miles before the storm had covered the tracks and hidden the scent from Otter's dogs. Blossom had already cut her hair and made deep cuts on her arms in mourning for her daughter's death.

After the bodies of the three hunters were laid out in the teepee of Stone Knife and Laughing Woman, the women of the village were cleaning them and dressing them in their finest ceremonial dress. Charging Bull called a council. Everyone in the village would have their say; something had to be done. They had to kill the bear or leave the valley where they had lived for generations. They had no other choices.

Red Hawk and Buffalo Heart had been standing guard on the far side of the village when Zach and the others came in. They were the last to know what had happened to the missing hunters. They were called in for the council; Charging Bull felt it was important that everyone in the village had an opportunity to speak their will at the council.

Zach was anxious after learning the grizzly had returned to the village and had taken Flower Song. The great bear had done that after driving the three hunters off the cliff. The tradition of the council could not be hurried, and although his patience was just about gone, he realized the pipe must be passed around the fire. The smoke from the sacred pipe must carry their prayers to the one above, the creator of all things.

Charging Bull asked Raven Wing to take Blue Fox's place around the council fire. After the pipe was put away, Charging Bull spoke, "This is a sad day for our people as we mourn the loss of Stone Knife, Broken Nose, Standing Deer, and Flower Song. Our village will not be the same without them. As a village we will mourn today and when the sun is straight overhead tomorrow, we will bury our dead. For this council today we will decide what we are going to do about the great killer bear.

Spotted Elk was filled with both anger and sorrow. As War Chief of his people he felt a great responsibility to keep them safe, but with this bear he had failed. There were now five Shoshone that the bear had taken from them and although he didn't know how, he vowed to himself, there would be no others. What bothered him the most was he did not know how to stop the bear any more than anyone else did. He finally spoke, "I have listened to the stories my brothers, Grizzly Killer and Running Wolf have told of the great bear they faced along a river far to the southwest of us. They told of our cousins from the Shoshone far to our west shooting their arrows and their arrows not doing more than barely going through its hide. To stop this bear it will take everyone with guns. Arrows will only make things worse."

Zach stood and spoke, saying, "Spotted Elk is right. The great grizzly he speaks of took a dozen shots from our rifles before he breathed no more and there were more Shoshone arrows in him than rifle balls. It will take all of us to stop this killer."

It was Ely that spoke next, "We've chased him with dogs and he killed the dogs, we've hunted the mountains and he has killed our horses and our warriors. We must be ready the next time he comes at us."

Zach nodded, agreeing with what Ely had said, but added, "It is not safe for hunters to go into the mountains unless we go in groups with rifles."

Everyone nodded but then Bear Heart looked at his old friend, Charging Bull, and said, "Charging Bull, remember when we were young and camped way up by the headwaters of the Seed-Kee-Dee? We were hunting sheep when the great bear killed two of our horses and drug off a sheep we had hanging." Charging Bull smiled, remembering that hunt so many years before. Bear Heart continued, "It was Soaring Eagle that had us dig pits and place sharpened sticks in the bottom so if the bear came back and fell in a pit he would impale himself on the sticks."

Charging Bull nodded, and said, "I remember old friend. I remember how you and I struggled with a large boulder while the older hunters laughed at us."

Bear Heart smiled as he nodded, then asked, "Do you believe that might work now?"

Zach had heard of people digging bear pits and heavy log traps for bears but he had never seen it done. It was decided they would dig pits on all of the trails coming from the mountains.

Raven Wing stood and slowly sprinkled a combination of several of the plants she kept into the fire, creating a smoke of several different shades of gray to nearly black. She had one of her crystals around her neck and she chanted a prayer that the smoke would carry to the heavens. Everyone in the village was silent, hoping their powerful new Shaman's medicine could protect them against the power of the great bear.

Chapter 23

Terror in the Night

BY THE TIME darkness had settled over the valley of the Wind River, the bodies of Stone Knife, his son Standing Deer, and brother Broken Nose had been cleaned up and dressed in their finest buckskins and head dresses. They were laid on buffalo robes along the outside walls of Stone Knife's teepee, leaving room for everyone in the village to walk around the small fire in the center and say farewell to these respected warriors.

They all believed these warriors and even little Flower Song would be with their ancestors very soon after they traveled the great trail of the Milky Way to their new home among the stars. Every person in the village, both young and old, made the slow procession through the teepee that evening. Laughing Woman and Singing Bird had both cut the long braids off their hair and blood still seeped from the wounds where, like Blossom, these two women had cut their arms and across their breasts in mourning. Blossom joined the other two for the night, sitting with the dead, knowing her child was gone and wishing they had found the body so she could be laid out with these men, all victims of the killer bear. The bodies would not be left alone until they reached their final resting place and then, along with their war horses, they would be laid to rest and covered with stones to keep the predators away from them. Blossom cried even more for her young daughter, knowing her bones would be scattered and her flesh eaten by the bear.

Raven Wing had taken some of Flower Song's belongings, her ceremonial dress and moccasins, and had placed one of her crystals where the child's heart would have been and prayed, asking the one above to find her lost soul and see that she finds her way into the land of her ancestors. Zach wasn't sure that what Raven Wing had done would really make any difference for he believed the child was already with those that had gone before her, but he was sure that her actions helped Blossom, the child's mother, and most everyone else in the village.

Zach, Running Wolf, and the other searchers had not slept at all the night before and they were all dead tired, but the village had to be protected. Most of the rifles in camp belonged to the men that had been with the searchers and they were the only ones that knew how to use the guns well enough to be effective with them. With no sleep at all, Zach kissed his wives and babies good night and headed out to the perimeter of the village with nearly every other able bodied man in the village to guard against the bear's return.

The next morning Charging Bull was seeing to the preparation of the burial site. He had chosen a small knoll about a mile east of the river. He had Red Hawk and Buffalo Heart get the war horses of the three from the herd so they would have their best mounts to ride as they make their journey to the other side.

Grizzly Killer had two other rifles he had taken over the years from different men that he had helped find their way into hell for the murder and thievery of friends. He had already given Spotted Elk, Red Hawk, and Buffalo Heart rifles years ago, but now he felt every rifle he owned needed to be in the hands of those protecting the village.

The next morning he gave one of them to High Back Bull and handed the other to Otter. Grub, Ely, and Benny took them out of the village to show them how to use the rifles and to practice with them. After shooting most of the balls they had molded they recovered the lead from the sand bank of the river they were shooting into and the three trappers patiently showed High Back Bull and Otter how to melt the lead and cast new balls for their rifles. They showed them how to clean the barrels and the flash holes so when they needed the rifle it would indeed shoot for them. Ely replaced the flints that were worn down on both rifles.

High Back Bull was now seventeen summers while Otter was twice that many in age. Both felt honored that Grizzly Killer had chosen them to carry the deadly rifles of the white man. Like Spotted Elk, Red Hawk, and Buffalo Heart, Otter and High Back Bull felt more confident than ever they could now stop the killer bear.

It was a sad and long procession as everyone in the village followed the bodies to the burial knoll. A travois had been put on each of their horses and their bodies laid out on them. Charging Bull lead the way, leading Stone Knife, Spotted Elk was next leading Broken Nose, and then it was High Back Bull leading Standing Deer. The line that followed stretched out for several hundred feet. Even Zach's twins were carried along.

The twins were the newest members of the tribe and to the Shoshone they represented the future of their people. Even though everyone knew they were only temporary residents of the village, they understood as the elders and warriors died there had to be births or their people would cease to exist. So the babies were honored and made a big part of the village from the moment they were born.

The entire village watched from around the small knoll as the bodies of the three were carefully laid in their prepared resting places. Then the three horses were killed alongside the warriors that they had carried into battle. The warriors along with their horses were then covered and rocks piled over them all to keep the bodies safe from animals.

After the burial ceremony, shifts were set up with the men to guard the village, as Zach and the others that hadn't slept got a few hours of much needed rest. Zach had no idea when the killer grizzly would be back but he felt sure they would be dealing with the big bear sometime in the near future. He, like everyone else, was worried for the safety of his family and friends, for he knew if the bear got inside the village more would die before they could stop this giant killer.

Another week passed with no sign of the bear. The hunters that went out each day stayed away from the Wind River Mountains all together, hunting the east side of the river and down toward the Sweetwater.

Another week passed and another full moon presented itself. Badua'-mea', the melting moon, April, had arrived. Zach, Running Wolf, and their friends had been doing some trapping but without going up along the streams and meadows of the Wind River Mountains the spring trapping season had not been a good one.

Five bear pits had been finished and covered with willow branches and dead leaves from last fall. Deer and Elk urine had been taken from the animals they hunted and sprinkled around the pits to cover the human scent, but no further sign of the bear had been seen.

As the days had gotten longer and warmer Zach and his family were all anxious to see their home on Black's Fork. He still felt the killer grizzly was a problem, and he didn't want to leave until he knew everyone in the village was safe, but now he like everyone else was wondering if the big bear had left the area for good.

Sun Flower, Shining Star, and Raven Wing were as anxious as Zach and Running Wolf to go back to their own land. The north slope of the Uintah's that most of the surrounding tribes were now calling the land of Grizzly Killer. To Zach it was simply home. It was the Uintah Mountains of the Ute Indians; it was where he had buried his Pa. It was where he had learned to survive this deadly wilderness and where he had learned to become a Mountain Man. It was home, much more so than Kentucky, where he was born and raised, had ever been. It was where he'd learned to love and where his first child was born and after being away for a year it was where he longed to be.

There was no reason to stay any longer if the great killer grizzly had moved on and was no longer threatening the village. It had been a full moon now since the bear had been seen that terrible night when he had taken little Flower Song.

Zach and Running Wolf with Jimbo, Grub, Ely, and Benny with their pups and Otter with his dogs, Red Hawk and Buffalo Heart with their pups, had all been along the foothills several times and there had been no sign of the bear. Zach still waited, he wanted to be sure, but when the moon showed only half full he announced to everyone that in three days' time, they would be leaving, going back to their home on Black's Fork.

Buffalo Heart had a look of sadness when Zach went to his teepee and told him, but as Zach was saying it would take a couple of days to get ready for the trip, the look on Buffalo Heart's face changed. He said, "Grizzly Killer, I have spent more time with you and your family over the last year than I have here and I do not want that to change. What would you and Running Wolf say if I go with you?"

Zach smiled and said, "Buffalo Heart, you have been my friend since you, Red Hawk, and Sees Far came to us all those years ago. You are and always will be welcome with us."

Buffalo Heart smiled. Now instead of sadness a look of excitement and adventure came over him and he said, "I will speak with my family and Charging Bull and tell them of my decision." Zach shook his hand then went on to Red Hawk and Meadowlark's teepee to tell him they were leaving.

Sun Flower, Shining Star, and Raven Wing had taken the little ones to see their grandparents and let Bear Heart and White Feather know the time had come for them to go back to their home. Although they all could see the sadness on the face of their mother, she knew this day was coming and that her daughters had lives of their own to live. They knew that both daughters had better lives with Grizzly Killer and Running Wolf than they ever could have had if they'd stayed in their own village. Even though they hated to see them go they were happy for them and the lives they were living.

Red Hawk was as sad as Buffalo Heart had been at hearing that Grizzly Killer and Running Wolf were leaving. Zach did not say anything to Red Hawk and Meadowlark about Buffalo Heart going with them; Zach felt Red Hawk should hear that from Buffalo Heart himself.

Zach and the women spent much of the next day working on their packs as Running Wolf and Buffalo Heart separated their horses from the herd and getting them used to the halters after running free all winter. There were a couple of them that had gotten down right rank from being loose and free through the cold months.

Most everyone in the village came by to say their farewells and Bear Heart and White Feather spent all day long with their grandchildren. High Back Bull and Otter both came by to return the rifles Zach had given them and both were shocked and grateful when he looked surprised and told them both that he had given them the rifles not just to let them borrow them.

Spotted Elk had gone out early that morning with several others hunting, for there was to be a farewell feast this last night before Grizzly Killer and his family left the village. They went south and found the first of the buffalo returning to their summer range. They took three young bulls and by early afternoon was back with the heavily laden pack horses they had taken with them.

As different as the Indian people were from the whites he had been raised among, they loved life and used any excuse to celebrate just as the whites did. They danced around the fires to the beat of the rawhide drums until way into the night, they ate and enjoyed the first fresh buffalo they'd had in weeks. Everyone told them how much they would be missed; even Benny and Little Dove hated to see them go. Grub and Ely understood Zach but even understanding, along with Benny, they hated to see them leave. They did expect to see them again in Willow Valley for the Rendezvous in just three short months.

It was well after midnight when the last of the outside fires had died down and the villagers were mostly asleep for the night. The guards around the village had been reduced to where now there were only three patrolling the perimeters each night.

Once back in the teepee, Zach gently kissed his sleeping children and then watched as his two beautiful wives slipped out of the doeskin dresses and by the dim light of the small fire he watched with delight as they laid down on the buffalo robe, waiting for him to get between them before pulling the heavy grizzly robe up over their naked bodies.

He laid down between them and reveled in the feeling as both women laid their head on his shoulders. Sun Flower was the first to fall asleep, her deep steady breathing telling him she was out until the little twins awoke. Only minutes later he could hear the soft snores of Jimbo curled up by the lodge opening. He felt Shining Star move and then her hand and fingers start to move on his chest slowly moving down his body, when her hand reach his waist he had started to get aroused, when suddenly Jimbo growled.

Just a moment later a rifle shot shattered the stillness and several dogs started barking. Jimbo pushed his way outside the teepee and Zach was instantly on his feet with rifle and possibles bag in hand and without taking time to dress or even pull on his moccasins he stepped out into the cool night air naked.

The moon was up, but at a little less than half full it wasn't a bright night. The fires around the village were now nothing more than glowing coals. Zach couldn't see what the dogs were upset about, then he heard one yelp and then silence. Even before the first yelp had faded another dog started screaming and Zach knew it was seriously hurt. He was now running toward the sounds of the dogs fighting. He could hear the vicious growls of Jimbo and that of a very mad bear. He was nearly upon them before he saw the giant grizzly. The bear had one of Jimbo and Luna's pups in his mouth and in the dim light Zach couldn't tell if it was alive or not. He shouldered his Hawken and fired, the bear was less than ten yards from him. He had aimed directly for its shoulder knowing the grizzly couldn't charge with a broken shoulder. The bear dropped the lifeless pup and spun biting at the wound. Zach was reloading when a flash of light just a few feet away caused him to close his eyes just as the boom of Running Wolf rifle split the night.

Zach was reloaded in less than a minute but by then four more shots had shattered the darkness, and still the bear stood up. His head was over half way to the top of the lodge poles of the teepees and he growled his anger at both the dogs and men surrounding him.

Zach fired again, along with Running Wolf, Benny, Grub, and Ely. The giant grizzly dropped back onto all fours and stumbled when his weight hit his broken shoulder. Red Hawk, Buffalo Heart, High Back Bull, and Otter all fired again and the bear slowly laid his massive head onto the ground. Another volley and the thick gray smoke hung in the air so thick it was impossible to tell if the giant bear was dead. Less than a minute later another eight shots were fired, Zach didn't believe that last volley was necessary, but he fired as well not willing to take a chance with a bear this big.

Even after the last volley was fired, everyone reloaded just as rapidly as they could. In the dark none of them could see the giant's eyes, to tell if he was dead. In the calm night air in took several minutes for the acrid powder smoke to clear. They then could plainly see the still form of the great silver tipped grizzly lying there before them.

No one was willing to approach the bear, not until they knew for sure he was dead. Zach was still naked along with about half of the others that had ran out to defend the village. In fact Grub and Ely were the only ones completely dressed. Neither of them removed their buckskins to sleep.

Zach could see four lifeless dogs lying around the bear. One of them was White Wolf the smallest of Jimbo and Luna's pups, but Jimbo was right by his side. He thought White Wolf, although smaller than the other pups, had a heart every bit as big. A fire was soon going just in front of where Zach was standing and Shining Star brought Zach his buckskins while Sun Flower cared for all three of their children as the gun shots had awakened them.

194

There was no sleeping for the rest of the night, the village was celebrating; the killer bear was dead. Killed by the power of the white man's guns. It was their white brother, Grizzly Killer that had stopped the bear from running with his first shot and it was High Back Bull that had warned the village with his first shot with the rifle given to him by Grizzly Killer. It was the great medicine dog and his pups that had kept the bear occupied until the long guns could kill him. The medicine of Grizzly Killer and his dog had proven more powerful than even the giant bear and the stories of this night and this bear would be told around the council fires and campfires of the Shoshone people for as long as the sun rises.

Chapter 24

Power of the Great Bear

AS EARLY MORNING light crept over the valley, everyone in the village came to look at the huge bear. Zach and Running Wolf had faced a giant killer bear a few years before down on Weber's River south of Willow Valley, but as they looked at this one they believed this was bigger than that thousand pound bear had been. Even the elders could not remember hearing tell of a bear this big and powerful, and they all believed it had been the powerful medicine of Grizzly Killer and his dog that had defeated the bear this night, without anyone else being killed by this huge beast.

The front paws were nearly a foot across and from his nose to his tail was over ten feet. The giant claws were as longer than Zach's longest finger and he believed the bear's bulk was more than that of Ol' Red and Ol' Red was bigger than any of the horses, except for the half Shire pack horse that Grub and Ely had.

Starting the journey back to Black's Fork was going to have to wait another day. They were all tired and the village would be celebrating all day. The giant had to be skinned and everyone felt the hide should be given to Grizzly Killer, but Zach shook his head and with Raven Wing standing by his side he said, "Charging Bull, this hide and the deadly claws belong

196

to the Shoshone people, not to just one man. It should be used for ceremonies and important councils, let it be a symbol of the strength of the people, so they will always remember that together they are strong but alone no one could have stopped the great bear."

Charging Bull nodded along with Spotted Elk, Bear Heart, and the other elders that were there. Charging Bull, spoke, "Grizzly Killer, your heart is that of a true Shoshone and you are wise beyond your years. The great bear will be a ceremonial robe, its claws will be given to each one of the great warriors that protected our village. His skull will rest above our council fire so our enemies will feel the power of the medicine of the Shoshone."

There were a dozen men that had started skinning the great grizzly. Like with a buffalo, they used horses and ropes to help strip the hide from the carcass. High Back Bull hadn't had any sleep for three days now but it was he that started in on the huge claws. It took him nearly five hours to dig out all of the claws and clean the ends to his satisfaction, he then presented them to Charging Bull. Charging Bull simply nodded as he took the huge claws, each one was longer than his longest finger.

He took the claws to Raven Wing and asked her if she would pray over them so that the men he was giving them too would feel the great medicine he believed they carried. Raven Wing unrolled a soft piece of elk hide and laid the claws out on it in the row. Between every fourth claw, she placed one of her sacred crystals. These were crystals that the mountain had given her a year ago along with the yellow gold that the white men thought was so valuable.

Charging Bull watched with interest as Raven Wing set the claws and crystals in a certain way. She then got out a small bundle of sweet sage and set it on the edge of the small fire. After the sage was smoking, she picked it up looked through the smoke hole watching the tendril of smoke twist and curl up and out of the teepee. She then closed her eye and started to chant.

> *O smoke from the sweet sage,*
> *carry our thoughts and prayers.*
> *O smoke from the sweet sage,*
> *carry our thoughts and prayers.*
> *O smoke from the sweet sage,*
> *open the heart of the one above.*
> *O smoke from the sweet sage,*
> *open the heart of the one above.*
> *Give the medicine of the great bear to*
> *those that carry this part of him.*
> *Give the medicine of the great bear to*
> *those that carry this part of him.*
> *We honor you, Great Spirit,*
> *as you have given us life to live.*
> *We honor you, Great Spirit,*
> *as you have given us this world to live on.*

Raven Wing stopped the chanting of her prayer but continued humming the rhythm she had been chanting. She still held the smoking bundle of sage and slowing moved it to the four cardinal directions and to the sky above and earth below. She then handed the smoldering bundle to Charging Bull and he, just as she had done, moved the sage in the four directions and to the sky and earth.

Once they were satisfied the claws carried the blessing of the one above and that they held the medicine of the great bear, Charging Bull thanked Raven Wing and added, "Know this Raven Wing, you will be missed, but all of our people wish you and all of your family a long and happy life."

He left her standing there with her emotions still mixed about leaving. Not that she had any doubts about it, she didn't, but her feelings were still mixed.

Charging Bull called a council for late that afternoon after Grizzly Killer and the others that hadn't slept for several nights had gotten a few hours of sleep. The spring storm had completely left the valley of the Wind River and the warm spring sun had melted the snow from the valley floor.

It was a group of very tired men, none of which were ready to be awake that started to gather around the council fire. Charging Bull had the huge heavy bear hide stretched out between two large posts that were buried three feet into the ground. The hide had not been fleshed, and it alone weighed a lot. Over the next week or maybe two the hide would be finished with its hair left on and tanned with the bears own brain into a soft ceremonial robe, which would be used only on occasions such as this.

Charging Bull waited until everyone was in place. He then unwrapped the sacred pipe. After filling the pipe with tobacco, he smoked and prayed and passed it to Spotted Elk on his left. This ceremony was the heart of every council of the people and no one ever seemed to be in a hurry. Even the children showed reverence during this prayer ceremony.

Once the sacred pipe had been rolled back up in its highly decorated leather wrap, Charging Bull laid out another wrap. No one knew what their Chief was doing, and all eyes were watching as he carefully untied the rawhide strap and unrolled the wrap exposing the twenty claws of the great bear. Charging Bull then opened up his heart to his people, telling them that these claws represent the power of the great bear and any man that carries one of them will carry the bear's powerful medicine with him. He went on and told his people about the prayer of Raven Wing as she asked the one above to bless these claws, and with the power of her crystals and through the smoke of the sweet sage he knew her prayer had been heard.

The first of these twenty claws will go to the ten men that stopped the great bear. The first and longest claw he presented to Grizzly Killer, the next went to Spotted Elk. Then, Running Wolf, Benny, Grub, and Ely were all presented one, next Red Hawk and Buffalo Heart, High Back Bull and Otter. For these men, this was the highest honor they could receive and each one of them was truly grateful. There were ten claws left. He presented one to High Eagle for the loss of his daughter Flower Song, another to Laughing Woman, and the next to Singing Bird for the bear had killed their men. Next, he presented one to Long Lance. Although Howling Dog had been shamed by his actions, his death by the bear was a shock to all of them and Long Lance accepted the claw from his old friend with gratitude and a tear in his eye.

There were six of the large claws left, four of those were a bit smaller from the outside of the bear's mighty paw. Charging bull had thought all afternoon what should be done with those claws. He hoped his decision would meet with the people's approval. Jimbo was sitting on his haunches next to Zach who was holding both of his nearly five-month-old twins. The Chief smiled at the babies as he walked up to Zach once again. Both babies looked Shoshone in every way but one, both of them had eyes that were the color of the sky like their father's.

Charging Bull spoke so everyone could hear him and said, "We have six of the claws from the great bear left. I present one of them to the Great Medicine Dog to add to the other six he now wears so proudly. With Zach's hands full he gave the claw to Sun Flower who promised it would be on his collar before they left the next morning.

Charging Bull then walked back over to Otter, and again said loud enough for all to hear, This is the last to be given this day, it is for Tracker, for a braver dog there has never been. Even after he was nearly killed by the bear he once again attacked to try to help our people. A cheer went up from everyone that was there but none cheered louder and harder than Zach did. Tracker wasn't there, he once again was recovering from the deep wounds on his side and shoulder.

Charging Bull held up the remaining claws and said, "The four remaining claws, one from each of the great bears feet will stay with his hide and skull, together they will show the strength we have as a people, the great bear hurt us but he did not defeat us for we are Shoshone.

As the sun dropped behind the mountain peaks to the west, bear meat was dripping fat into every fire throughout the village. For the next several days the giant grizzly's fat would be rendered into lard and used for cooking, lotion, and even as a dressing for their hair. For tonight, the bear was providing a farewell feast for tomorrow Zach, Running Wolf, and their wives along with Buffalo Heart would be leaving the valley of the Wind River.

Chapter 25

Heading Home

ZACH WENT TO SLEEP early that night; the lack of sleep over the last several days had caught up with him. Shining Star and Sun Flower had been busy, but both stopped to smile at the sight of their big strong husband sound asleep with a twin in each arm and Star lying on his chest. All four of them were fast asleep.

Shining Star had heated the end of one of their sewing awls and carefully burned a hole through both of the grizzly claws that Charging Bull had given to Zach that day. While she was doing that Sun Flower was making another loop to hold the claw on Jimbo's collar. Once she was satisfied it would hold the claw securely, she handed it to Shining Star to add the claw to his already impressive collar of six grizzly claws and a piece of turquois that he had carried for years. The other went on Zach's necklace, the famous grizzly claw necklace that even those that didn't know him, recognized him by that necklace. He was known everywhere he went by the necklace he always wore.

Red Hawk had been distraught ever since Buffalo Heart had told him he was leaving with Grizzly Killer to live with them on Black's Fork. Since the two of them were born only months apart nineteen summers ago, they had never been apart.

They were closer than most brothers were and Meadowlark, as much as she loved Red Hawk, could see her husband would never be happy with his best friends gone. She knew, besides Buffalo Heart, that Grizzly Killer and Running Wolf were his closest friends, she knew she would never be able to take the place of a lifetime of friendship.

Red Hawk was quiet, not even getting excited like he usually did as she slipped out of her dress and pressed her naked body up against his. When he didn't want to make love, she knew the only way she could keep him happy was if they too left their home and went to live in the land of Grizzly Killer with their friends.

She didn't say anything to him she just waited until she thought he was asleep then she quietly left their teepee and went to the lodge of Grizzly Killer. Jimbo didn't growl as she gently knocked and then whispered. Jimbo licked Zach's face, and he was instantly awake. Only moments later Meadowlark was sitting with Zach, Sun Flower, and Shining Star telling them of how Red Hawk felt and of her fears.

When Zach spoke, tears started to run down Meadowlark's cheeks, as he said, "First of all, Meadowlark, if you and Red Hawk would like to come with us you are more than welcome. There is room for many lodges at our home on Black's Fork, and we would all be safer there with a warrior as great as Red Hawk with us. However, if you wish to stay I am sure Red Hawk will just need time. He will make new friends."

She shook her head. "There are no friends like Buffalo Heart, you, and Running Wolf here and I know he would be much happier if we went with you."

Sun Flower spoke next, and she asked, "What about you, Meadowlark? What do you want to do?"

"I want to make my husband happy. My home is with him. You left our village for a man and so did Raven Wing, and so did you Shining Star. I will find happiness like you have with my man." Both women smiled knowing she was right and knowing that she truly did love Red Hawk.

Long before daylight first crept across the valley, Red Hawk had been to the horse herd and separated his string of horses. Since giving Wind in His Face his five best horses for his wife he only had three besides his own buffalo runner and the small mare that Meadowlark rode. Meadowlark had their lodge down and everything they owned ready to pack when he led the three horses up to where their lodge had stood. They still had not told anyone they were going, and they both knew it would be a shock to the village, but they both felt this was the right thing for them to do.

The hint of gray was starting to show along the eastern horizon when Red Hawk opened the flap and stepped inside the small teepee that he and Buffalo Heart had shared for the last couple of years. Buffalo Heart was just waking up but the surprise of seeing Red Hawk throwing sticks on the small fire in the dark made him ask, "What are you doing? Why are you not in bed with Meadowlark?"

"We are going with you, my friend. After I went to sleep Meadowlark went and talked to Grizzly Killer, Sun Flower, and Shining Star. When she came back, she woke me up and said we were going to Black's Fork with the rest of you."

"Does everyone else know?"

"No, you are the first we've told. Everyone else is still sleeping."

Red Hawk and Meadowlark had everything packed by the time the village started to stir. Buffalo Heart as well had his belongings put on two of his horses, his other four where strung together behind those two.

Basket Maker, Meadowlark's mother, was the first to see her daughter's lodge was gone. She just stood there still and silent as she saw her daughter and her husband helping Grizzly Killer and Running Wolf loading their horses.

Although her heart was filled with sadness, she knew her daughter was happy and was making a life of her own. Only a moment later Meadowlark saw her mother standing there and she went to her to explain, but Basket Maker stopped her, and she smiled and said, "You do not have to explain my daughter.

I know it is time you and Red Hawk go and make a life of your own."

Before Meadowlark could answer, Wind in His Face came up to them. He had a grave and dark look about him and the joy she felt this morning turned to apprehension. That apprehension was short lived as Red Hawk walked up just as Wind in His Face started to speak. The old and young warrior stood there facing each other. Both women were silent, neither knowing what was going to happen. Wind in His Face said, as both a question and a statement, "You are taking my daughter away from us?"

Red Hawk stood tall and proud as he answered, "Yes, we are going to make our home in the land of Grizzly Killer."

Wind in His Face didn't know what to say. He knew Red Hawk had every right to take Meadowlark wherever he wanted to. He himself had accepted Red Hawk's horses for his daughter which meant she now belonged to him. He felt both the sadness of loss and the joy of seeing his daughter go out on her own as he stood there. Red Hawk, Meadowlark, and Basket Maker were all silent staring at him, waiting for his response when Charging Bull walked up to them.

He had already been with Grizzly Killer, Buffalo Heart, and Running Wolf, and he knew another one of his young warriors was leaving. He, just like Wind in His Face, had mixed emotions. He hated to see them leave the village, but he was happy for them. They were going with Grizzly Killer to make a life of their own. Charging Bull had no doubt at all that in the village of Grizzly Killer they would find both happiness and security in which to raise their family. The Chief spoke, "Red Hawk, Meadowlark, know that you will be missed, but know too, you go with my love and my respect.

Wind in His Face had still not spoken and finally Meadowlark stepped forward and hugged her father. Although he knew this day would come, he felt like it had come much too soon. It seemed like just yesterday she was suckling at her mother's breast and now she was leaving with her own man for a life of her own. He finally looked back at Red Hawk and held his hand out to the nervous young man. He gripped Red Hawk's hand and arm and nodded but still never said a word. Wind in His Face finally said, "Go now, my children. Go and make your new home in the land of Grizzly Killer."

Wind in His Face and Basket Maker stood beside their Chief as Grizzly Killer, Running Wolf, and their families finished packing their string of horses. Jimbo, Luna, and their two pups Little Bear and Medicine Wolf were all running around anxious to be on the trail.

Grub, Ely, Benny and Little Dove were watching along with the rest of the villagers as Zach and Running Wolf tightened the diamond hitches over the packs on the horses. The packs would be secure as they headed south for the two hundred mile journey to their home on Black's Fork.

Zach figured it was about the middle of April; some buds were just starting to open on the willows along the river. It was spring in the Rockies; the grass was starting to green up and the days of sunshine was warm and pleasant. He figured the leaves would be coming out on the cottonwoods along the Seeds-Kee-Dee and the lower reaches of Black's Fork by the time they reached there. A week, he figured, maybe a little more, and the excitement of seeing home again after being away for a full year was making him want to hurry even more.

The farewells were said, and with the simple act of Zach pointing south, Jimbo led the way and they were on the trail once again to their home on the banks of Black's Fork on the north slope of the rugged Uintah Mountains. None of them were aware of the danger that awaited them when they arrived.

Other Books by Lane R. Warenski

About the Author

Lane R Warenski lives in a log home in Duchesne County, Utah, where he has an unrestricted view of the highest peaks in the mighty Uinta Mountains. He was raised being proud of his pioneer heritage and with a deep love and respect of the outdoors. Ever since childhood, following his father, Warenski has hunted, fished, and camped the mountains of the West. Whether it was the daily journals of William Ashley and Jedediah Smith or the fictional stories written by the great storytellers like Louis L'Amour and Terry C. Johnston, throughout his life, Warenski loves reading the history of the first explorers that came west, most of whom never dreamed they were opening this wild and rugged land to the pioneers and settlers that followed.

Find more great titles by Lane R Warenski and Wolfpack Publishing at www.wolfpackpublishing.com/lanerwarenski/